KATE FORSYTH

THE IMPOSSIBLE QUEST

2

WOLVES OF THE WITCHWOOD

Kane Miller
A DIVISION OF EDC PUBLISHING

Map of Wolfhaven & Surrounding Lands

The Witchwood

Crowthorne Castle

Blackmoor Bog

Rosemoran River

FOR BEN, TIM AND ELLA,
IN MEMORY OF CHILDHOOD GAMES

First American Edition 2016
Kane Miller, A Division of EDC Publishing

Text copyright © Kate Forsyth 2014

First published by Scholastic Press, a division of Scholastic Australia Pty Limited in 2014.
Cover illustration and map by Jeremy Reston.
Logo design by blacksheep-uk.com.
This edition published under license from Scholastic Australia Pty Limited.
Internal photography: brick texture on page i © GiorgioMagini|istockphoto.com;
castle on page iv and folios © ivan-96|istockphoto.com; skull on page 14 © Frankie Lee
|istockphoto.com; rings on page 145 © Czalewski|Dreamstime.com; wolf head as section
break © Tronin Andrei|shutterstock.com.

For information contact:
Kane Miller, A Division of EDC Publishing
P.O. Box 470663
Tulsa, OK 74147-0663
www.kanemiller.com
www.edcpub.com
www.usbornebooksandmore.com

Library of Congress Control Number: 2015938800

Printed and bound in the United States of America

3 4 5 6 7 8 9 10

ISBN: 978-1-61067-415-7

BANNERS »
« OF FLAME

Hours had passed since midnight, but Tom wouldn't let anyone rest. Stumbling, he led the way as fast as he dared down a steep road, slippery with mud. The landscape was bleak, with jagged rocks looming on either side. There was nowhere to hide.

His wolfhound whined, one foot lifted.

"Never mind, Fergus." Tom rubbed the dog's rough head. "We'll reach the Witchwood soon. Hopefully Lord Mortlake won't be able to find us there."

"He'll be too busy trying to stop his castle from burning down," Sebastian said. He turned and waved back towards the mountains. "Look, you can see the glare of the fire from here!"

Tom glanced back, and saw the night sky behind them lit up by a sullen red glow. He grinned.

"I can't believe we actually did it," said Quinn. Her voice rang with triumph, despite her weariness. "We beat him. We escaped Frostwick—"

"And we rescued the unicorn," Elanor murmured. She bent to pat the unicorn's arched neck and he gently tossed his wild black mane.

Tom's grin widened. He gazed at the unicorn pacing ahead, a huge dark shape in the shadows. He could just see the two girls on the beast's back, slumped with exhaustion. The darkness was lifting, the stars fading. Soon the night's protective cloak would disappear completely.

"We have to get a move on," Tom reminded them. "Lord Mortlake will be after us just as soon as he can. He'll want us . . . and he'll want his unicorn back."

"It's not *his*," said Elanor. "A unicorn belongs to no one."

"To think Lord Mortlake was going to slaughter him, just for his horn," Quinn added.

"But what if *we* have to do the same?"

Sebastian asked.

"We can't kill him," Quinn protested.

"I won't let it happen!" Elanor added, sitting up.

"But the prophecy says we need the unicorn's *horn*," Sebastian said. "We have to bring it together at dawn with a dragon's tooth, some kind of feather, and—"

"A *griffin* feather," Quinn said. "Don't you remember?"

"Not much of it," Sebastian admitted. "It feels like a month since we heard it all."

Tom had a flash of memory. The sinister shapes of the skeletal, leathery bog-men sneaking through the darkness, the flash of swords, the screams of the dying, his mother's defiant eyes as she faced the black-clad knight with boar tusks on his helmet. The knight who would soon be on their trail. Lord Mortlake.

He shivered, hoping his mother was unharmed. She'd been so brave. He hated to think what she might be suffering now, held prisoner by the bog-men, at the mercy of Lord Mortlake and his soldiers. Tom's resolve hardened. He had to rescue her and the rest of the prisoners of Wolfhaven Castle.

Even if it meant they had to kill the unicorn?

"The rhyme is a jumble now," Elanor said. "All I can remember is something about a wolf lying down with a wolfhound."

"And we need a dragon's tooth," Sebastian said. "I can picture myself as a dragon slayer!"

Tom screwed up his face, trying to remember the words of the Grand Teller, the witch of Wolfhaven Castle, who'd sent them on this wild quest. "Wasn't there something about the stones of the castle singing?"

Quinn sat up straight on the unicorn's back and began chanting:

WHEN THE WOLF LIES DOWN WITH THE WOLFHOUND
AND THE STONES OF THE CASTLE SING,
THE SLEEPING HEROES SHALL WAKE FOR THE CROWN
AND THE BELLS OF VICTORY RING.

GRIFFIN FEATHER AND UNICORN'S HORN,
SEA SERPENT SCALE AND DRAGON'S TOOTH,
BRING THEM TOGETHER AT FIRST LIGHT OF DAWN,
AND YOU SHALL SEE THIS SPELL'S TRUTH.

"How are we meant to find all those things?" Elanor said. "Who knows if they even exist? It's hopeless."

"Well, we thought finding a unicorn was hopeless too," said Tom, glancing at the horned beast. "We'll find all the others too. Don't worry, Ela."

"I hope so," she answered. "Because if we don't, we have no home, no family, no friends, and—"

"You shouldn't talk like that," Sebastian said. "A warrior never worries, don't you know?"

"I'm scared too," Quinn admitted. She glanced apprehensively over her shoulder, then jerked upright. "Oh no, look!"

The orange glow on the far horizon had spread and separated, and now raced towards them like a river of lava. It was a horde of men on horseback, galloping hard, the fiery torches in their hands streaming behind them like banners of flame.

2

»→ THE »————→
WITCHWOOD

"**R**un!" Quinn cried. Tom and Sebastian broke into a stumbling jog. Quinn held down her hand to them. "Get up on the unicorn!"

"There's no room!" Tom shouted. "And he can't carry all of us!"

"He's huge! Come on, the Witchwood isn't far. We just need him to carry us in under the trees."

Somehow the girls managed to drag Tom and Sebastian up, and Elanor kicked the unicorn into a canter. Fergus loped along beside them, as the road fell down between two tall ridges of rock.

"Look, there's the Witchwood!" Quinn cried. In the gray light of dawn the Witchwood undulated away as far as her eye could see, green and shadowy. The gnarled trunks that overhung the road were draped in velvety moss, their roots snaking away into darkness.

"Slow him down," Sebastian shouted. "We'll all be knocked off if he gallops under those low branches."

Elanor yanked on the reins with all her strength, and the unicorn slowed to a stop. The children slid off his back, landing with a thump on the road.

Quinn looked behind her. The line of flaming torches now looked like a great fiery serpent, slithering down the hill.

"Quick, into the trees!" Tom ordered. "And try not to leave any footsteps in the mud." He scrambled over the ditch that separated the road from the forest, Fergus leaping after him. Quinn followed quickly.

"Come on!" Sebastian had jumped across and now turned and held out his hand for Elanor. She took it and picked her way through the mud, making a face as her golden slippers squelched. She pulled on the reins and the unicorn leapt after her, landing nimbly under the trees then striding forward eagerly. He seemed happy leading them through the secret closes of the wood; his ears were pricked forward, his feathered hooves lifted high. The children had to half run to keep up with him.

In moments, the unicorn had led them away from the road, finding a narrow path that wound its way through the towering trunks of the trees, hung with vines of ivy. Mist moved in long streamers like the breath of some hidden monster, touching the backs of their necks with clammy fingers.

Quinn felt a delicious shiver of mystery and strangeness.

"Let's get as far away from the road as we can," Tom said. "Hurry."

They scrambled over mossy boulders and fallen trees, following the unicorn through the tangle of bracken and brambles.

"Shh, listen," Quinn said.

They all stopped, fists clenched and faces tense. Far behind them they heard the pound of hooves. Everyone dropped to the ground, crouching behind trees. Sebastian drew his sword and held it ready. Tom raised an arrow to his bow. The unicorn stood motionless, horn held high. With his dun-brown coat and black tail, he was almost invisible in the shadowy forest.

The hooves came closer and closer. Elanor pressed her face into her knees, covering her head with her arms. Quinn put her hand on the wolfhound's muzzle, keeping him quiet.

Through the trees they saw the distant flicker of flame. The smell of smoke belched towards them.

Then the riders galloped right past them, along the road, heading south.

The beat of hooves receded. Slowly they faded away.

Sebastian stood up and sheathed his sword again.

"Come on, let's get moving before they realize they've lost us," Tom said.

As fast as they could, the four children headed east, deep into the Witchwood.

"We have to be careful not to get lost in here," Quinn said, after a while. "We need to look out for the Hagburn. It's the only true landmark in the whole forest."

Elanor gazed into the woods with wide eyes. "The Hagburn? They haven't burned witches to death in here, have they?"

"Oh, no," Quinn answered. "The Hagburn is the name for the river that winds through here. 'Burn' means river or stream. And 'hag' is an old word that means 'bog.' It just means it's a boggy river."

"I've never heard a *bog* called a *hag*," Sebastian said. "Only ugly old witches."

Quinn scowled at him. "Not all witches are ugly and old."

"All the ones I've ever known were," Sebastian answered.

"Oh, and you're such an expert," Quinn retorted. "I'll have you know that I'll be a witch myself soon. I just need to win my witch's staff."

"Very well then," Sebastian responded, "not all witches are *old*!" He turned and laughed at Quinn's furious face, but she just kept on walking.

"I've heard tales of a witch in these woods," Tom said. "One who grinds human bones for bread."

"That was just a story to scare small children,"

said Quinn, shaking her head.

"So it's not true?" Elanor asked Quinn. "There's no witch in these woods? But isn't that why this is called the Witchwood?"

"It's highly likely there is one," Quinn answered. "There are always witches in forests—they love the wild, dark places. I just mean the witch would not grind bones for bread, my lady."

"There are wolves in this forest too," Tom said. "Big ones."

"And bears," Sebastian added.

"Bears?" Elanor repeated timidly.

"And all of them *hungry*," Sebastian added. He raised up both arms, spread his fingers like talons and made a growling sound deep in his throat. Elanor couldn't help smiling.

"*Soooo* frightening," Tom mocked. "I'm shaking in my boots."

Sebastian cast him an angry look. "Pot boy," he muttered under his breath.

On they hurried, leaving the road far behind them.

The sun was almost directly overhead when Quinn heard the babble of water. "This way," she said.

Scratched and bruised, they forced their way through to a small fast-moving river, cascading over stones.

"It's the Hagburn," Quinn said. "If we follow it, we're less likely to get lost."

Elanor made her way over the rocks and knelt to scoop water into her mouth. The others joined her. Fergus slurped noisily, and the unicorn dipped his head and drank too.

Farther up the Hagburn they found a clearing by a wide pool of water. Dragonflies hovered above the sparkling water, and birds twittered in the willow trees. Sebastian found an armful of fallen branches, while the others gathered twigs and leaves and dry moss to use as kindling.

Quinn thought it was strange seeing Lady Elanor,

daughter of the Lord of Wolfhaven Castle, with her green silk dress kilted above her knees, its hem heavy with mud, her browny-gold hair all in a tangle and her arms filled with twigs.

So much had changed so quickly, it was like living in a whirlwind. Quinn never seemed to find a moment to catch her breath, to stop and think. She wished with all her heart that Arwen was there to advise her.

A fire was soon burning, and the four children sat in a circle around it. They toasted sausages on long sticks and sipped hot tea made by boiling water with a handful of herbs.

"What now?" Elanor asked.

"We go in search of dragons!" said Sebastian, giving his sword a rub with the hem of his jacket.

"I think I should read the tell-stones," Quinn said. She opened the small leather bag at her waist and drew out four small white stones, all with silver marks. She laid them, one by one, at the four points of the compass, then looked to see what stones she had drawn.

"The first stone is Apple," she said. "That means fruition, or some kind of success."

"That's a good sign, right?" Elanor said hopefully.

"It's probably about finding the unicorn," Tom said, looking with pride at the horned beast cropping grass at one side of the clearing.

"The second stone is a Crescent Moon. That's a sign of new magic, intuition, and feminine energy, and often stands for a witch. It might be a sign for me," Quinn said. "Telling me to use my intuition."

"You're not a witch yet," Sebastian said.

Quinn glared at him. She didn't want anyone to know, but it hurt her to be teased. She wanted to be a full-fledged witch so badly, but the Grand Teller was always telling her she needed to be patient. *The time will come when you are ready*, Arwen always said. *How will I know?* Quinn would demand. The Grand Teller would only smile in her enigmatic way and say, *You will know.*

Quinn looked at the stone in the south position. It had three snaking lines. "Waves," she said. "The ebb and flow of energy means change. Waves bring things to you, and waves take them away."

"Let's hope it's bringing us a sea serpent," Sebastian said.

"Or a griffin," Tom said. "More likely to be found in a forest than a sea serpent, I think."

"I wonder if it means we should follow the river to its source," Quinn said. "It's meant to be a hidden place of magic and mystery."

She then looked at the fourth stone, everyone's eyes following hers. Nobody said a word. They had seen that stone before. It was the sign of the Skull.

Darkness. Danger. Death.

3

← «SLAP,» →
SLAP, SLAP

Sebastian stared at the tell-stone, his stomach sinking. He imagined his father scoffing at him, sitting around and consulting some old witch magic. Lord Aiden would tell them to get moving and find something to fight. *Valor, Glory, Victory!* he would shout. *Live by the sword and die by the sword!*

Slap, slap, slap . . .

Fergus sat up, growling.

Slap, slap, slap, slap . . .

Sebastian's head jerked around. He stood up, a sudden sharp twist of fear in his gut.

Fergus was snarling, all the hair on his back standing up in a ridge. The unicorn was pawing one hoof uneasily, eyes wide and ears laid back. Quinn was on her feet too, her face as white as whey.

Sebastian peered through the gloom. It was dim as dusk under the towering trees of the Witchwood. Sebastian could see nothing but looping vines and shadowy ferns overhanging the wide brown pool of water.

Tom jumped up, seizing his bow. "It's the bog-men!"

Quinn clutched the wooden medallion she wore around her neck. "They must've tracked our scent!"

Elanor's eyes widened and she stared out into the forest. "Are you sure?" Then she heard the *slap, slap, slap* of leathery feet moving fast. She scrambled up, seizing hold of the unicorn's bridle. The beast shied nervously, and she soothed him as best as she could. "We must flee," she said. "They're so close!"

"We'll have to fight them off," Sebastian said, grabbing his sword and buckling it at his waist. "Get behind me, Lady Elanor."

"No, we can't fight them," Tom said impatiently. "They move in packs, there'll be too many of them. We have to run."

"But can we outrun them?" Quinn said, snatching her belongings and cramming them into her knapsack. "They move so fast!"

"You and Elanor get up on the unicorn," Tom ordered. "Sebastian and I will try and fight them off so you two can get away."

"No," Quinn snapped, drawing both her daggers. "We're sticking together."

The unicorn neighed and stamped his hooves, shaking his long mane. Elanor tried to hold him, but he tossed his head, almost knocking her to the ground.

Tom rushed to help her, but Sebastian shouldered him out of the way. "I'll hold him," he said, grabbing the reins.

"Don't let him go," Tom said to Sebastian. "We can't lose him. Lead him into the pool. The water will wash away our scent."

Sebastian scowled. There was nothing he hated more than that skinny pot boy ordering him around. "No, I think—" he began.

"Don't argue with me! We don't have time! Quinn, tie the knapsacks to the unicorn's back."

She obeyed at once.

Boiling with rage, Sebastian led the unicorn into the pool.

"Elanor, grab some pebbles," Tom said, kicking dirt over the fire.

"Why?"

"Just trust me," Tom pleaded.

Elanor bent and picked up some river pebbles from beside the water. Her narrow face was pale. "You want me to throw them at the bog-men?" she asked.

"No. Rub your hands all over them, then run down that path and throw them as far as possible. Then walk back in your own footsteps, the best you can. We want to throw them off our scent, make them think we've gone that way."

She nodded, running along the narrow, twisty path that led away from the pool and over the writhing roots of the trees. She flung the rocks down the path, as far away as she could. They landed just a few feet away and Tom threw up his hands, frustrated.

Elanor then made her way to the pool backward, stepping in the smudged marks her slippers had made in the mud. By the time she reached the campsite, Sebastian was knee-deep in the water, the unicorn dragging against the reins, turning to listen.

The sound of running feet came closer. Fergus snarled, his shaggy ears raised, hair bristling down his spine. "Quiet, boy," said Tom.

The unicorn reared, neighing. Elanor ran to him. "Shh," she whispered, stroking his velvety nose.

Sebastian caught sight of a flicker of movement. A sticklike figure was crawling over the tangled roots of the trees, his leathery face bent down low to the ground. At the sound of the unicorn's neigh, the creature lifted its head, then made a sharp *tat-tat-tat* with the end of its spear on a tree root. At once, two dozen bog-men swarmed out of the forest, spears held high. A swirl of foul-smelling mist roiled over their skulls.

"Quick, into the water," Tom whispered, hoisting his longbow and quiver above his head in the hope he could keep them dry. They all waded deep into the pool, Elanor and Quinn clinging to the unicorn's long black mane. Tom came last, Fergus dog-paddling faithfully behind.

Soon the water was above their knees, and then, with only a few more steps, up to their waists. It was shockingly cold. Another step, and the ground disappeared under their feet. Sebastian almost sank, struggling to keep his sword from getting wet. The unicorn struck out with his hooves, swimming forward. They all clung to his neck and back, moving away from the clearing and towards the far end of the pool, hidden in the shadows of a low-hanging tree. The wolfhound swam behind them, holding his head high, water arrowing behind him.

Finally, Sebastian felt his toes brushing against rocks again. He put his feet down, and Tom found his footing beside him. Elanor and Quinn were not tall enough to stand, but they clung to the unicorn's neck. Fergus reached the far shore and scrambled out, shaking himself vigorously. Water flew from his shaggy coat, drenching them all, but no one flinched. They were all staring back at the clearing, scarcely daring to breathe.

The bog-men crawled out of the shadows, lit up by a slanting ray of sunshine. Each seemed made from sticks or bones, wrapped in black, ancient leather. Their eyes were empty sockets; their skeletal hands gripped long, thin spears made of dark wood.

Blindly they crept forward, smelling the ground where the children and their dog had rested, investigating the hot ashes of the fire. Most were tall as men; some, though, were smaller even than Elanor. Some seemed to have old wounds in their heads or sides. One had only a single arm; another dragged a crippled leg. All had hideous mouths in which only a few yellow, broken teeth remained.

Sebastian and his friends all stayed as quiet as they could. Even the unicorn made no sound, standing as still as a statue, only the flaring of his nostrils and the flicker of his thick, black eyelashes showing he was alive.

I hope they are as blind as they seem, Sebastian thought. *Because if they simply glanced this way, they would surely see us.*

The eyeless faces were bent low to the ground, their nostrils flaring.

One of the bog-men caught the scent of Elanor's

feet along the path. It rapped its spear end sharply on a tree trunk, then scrambled away from the clearing. All the others swarmed after it, flat feet slapping on the mud.

Sebastian hated to admit it, but Tom's ruse had worked. *He's clever*, Sebastian admitted grudgingly to himself. For some reason, this made him even madder.

When the last hideous creature had slithered out of sight, Tom urgently gestured to the others to move upriver. "Quick! They'll be snuffling after us again in no time!"

4

QUICKTHORN

The Witchwood was a dark and sinister place. The river was overhung with trailing vines, and the trees grew thick and gnarled like old warriors. Birds rose up from the undergrowth with a clapping of wings. Elanor felt as if eyes were watching her, as if nostrils were sniffing her scent. Every crackle and crunch made her jump; every sigh and swish made her skin creep.

"Are they following us?" she whispered.

"Looks like we tricked them," Tom said. Then, as Elanor reached for a trailing vine, he cried, "But don't touch anything! They know your scent."

"Let's put her back on the unicorn," Sebastian suggested. "They'll find her harder to track then."

Being back on the unicorn made her feel much safer. Elanor bent and wrapped her arms around the beast's strong neck, burying her face in his long black mane. The unicorn smelled like the forest, of damp leaves, rich earth and the sharp scent of wood sorrel.

Not ten minutes had passed before they heard the menacing *slap, slap, slap* of feet behind them again, and then an urgent *tat-tat-tat*. Elanor saw the flickering shapes of bog-men running through the trees behind them. "They've found us," she cried.

"We have to move faster," Sebastian urged. But it was too late. A pack of bog-men suddenly leapt upon them. Bony fingers reached for Elanor, dragging her down from the unicorn. The smell of rot and decay engulfed her. She fought back as best she could, pulling free the knife she wore at her belt and jabbing all around her. The unicorn whinnied and came to her rescue, stabbing with his glinting horn, flailing with sharp-edged hooves, while the others fought with the same desperation. Sebastian's sword was swinging, Tom's arrows were whizzing past her ears, Fergus was growling and leaping and biting, and Quinn was slashing with both her daggers, one silver and one black.

The bog-men fought on, dragging the arrows out of their bodies, letting their injured limbs dangle uselessly. They didn't scream, or grunt, or gasp. They didn't bleed. They simply raised their spears once more and crawled forward. Soon, the four children were forced into a circle, fighting back-to-back.

The unicorn's spiraling black horn pierced one of their attackers clean through the chest. The bog-man fell and did not rise again. Wisps of smoke rose up from the gaping wound. Slowly flames licked up, and the smell of burning hide filled the air.

Again and again the unicorn stabbed, and each time the bog-men fell and began to smoke. Soon there was nothing left but a ring of eyeless skulls and ash.

Elanor found it hard to catch her breath. The acrid vapor stung her eyes and caught in her throat.

"Let's get away from here," Sebastian said, glancing down at a bloody slash on his forearm. "More will be here, any second!"

"We need to get away from the river, it's too easy for them to find us by following it." Tom gathered up his arrows. "Let them think we've waded upstream."

He jammed all the arrows into his quiver, then took river pebbles, rubbed them all over, and threw them as far as he could, in every direction. Elanor, Quinn and Sebastian all did the same, then Elanor and Quinn climbed up onto the unicorn.

"I wouldn't have thought the unicorn could do that," Elanor said.

"Kill the bog-men?" Quinn replied, her voice low. "He is a wild beast, after all, and his horn is his weapon."

"Lucky for us," Sebastian said, scrambling up the path beside them. "Else we'd all be dead."

"And it's not like the bog-men are alive, really," said Tom.

Elanor nodded. Though they ran and fought, the bog-men seemed like something that had been dead for centuries. The unicorn had simply let them return to the earth, she told herself.

The path twisted and turned, disappeared and reappeared, tilted up and pitched low. Roots squirmed like snakes, tripping the children. Only the unicorn trod lightly and easily, head held high.

Elanor felt thorns ripping at her skin, creepers seeking to drag her down. She pressed herself as close to the unicorn as she could.

At last, panting, Tom flung himself down on a rock. Elanor slid off the unicorn and knelt beside him, scanning the path with anxious eyes. "Do you think we've thrown them off our trail?"

"I hope so," Tom said.

"Let's keep going," Quinn said.

The boys nodded and began to run, and the unicorn lengthened his stride. Fergus loped along at his heels.

The sun was sinking in the sky, the shadows stretching long, when finally no one could run any farther. All afternoon, they had taken turns riding the unicorn, but it had been a long night and an even longer day, and all four were utterly worn out. Even the unicorn seemed exhausted.

They came at last to a grove of hawthorn trees, old and dusted with the snow of the last of their blossoms.

"Let's stop here," Quinn said. "Hawthorns are

magical trees and they will protect us."

Sebastian tried to barge through and found himself snagged by thorns on all sides. "I guess the thorns will keep any wild beasts away, at least," he grumbled.

"Not to mention the bog-men," added Tom, crawling in under the thorns.

Elanor slipped sideways past the thorns and found herself within a small green grove. The unicorn stepped softly through the trees and stood cropping the grass, his hide almost exactly the same color as the dappled silvery trunks of the thorn trees. Fergus lay down, head on paws, ears relaxed.

"See, the animals think we'll be safe here," Quinn said, sitting down. "Arwen says that the hawthorn is a faerie tree and will always guard the innocent of heart. She calls it the Whitethorn tree, or sometimes, the Quickthorn."

"My mam calls it the bread-and-cheese tree," Tom said, as he began to pluck the fresh young leaf buds. "Because the buds taste so good. Here, try one." He popped one in his mouth, then tossed one to each of the other three. Sebastian caught it instinctively, but then stared at it in disgust and tossed it away.

Quinn tentatively nibbled it, then her face lit up. "It's good!"

Elanor tasted her leaf bud gingerly, then smiled at Tom. "It's delicious!"

Tom began to pick dandelion leaves and more hawthorn buds. "Why don't you make us a fire?" he said to Sebastian.

Sebastian scowled. "I don't think that's a good idea. The bog-men will smell the smoke and find us."

"Hawthorn burns with hardly any smoke," Tom said. "But suit yourself. No fire means no hot supper."

Sebastian's scowl deepened. Then he got up with a loud *huff!* He drew his sword, preparing to hack down a few branches.

"Don't cut the green wood!" Tom and Quinn cried at the exact same moment. They grinned at each other, then Quinn said, "It's bad luck."

"And it'll smoke," Tom added.

Sebastian stamped off to find fallen wood, and Elanor ran to help him. Their tinder was all wet, so they had to scrape moss off the tree trunks and gather dead grass, leaves and bits of dead bark, piling them high. Sebastian then tried to strike a spark from the steel and flint, but only managed a few stray flickers.

Tom groaned impatiently, grabbed the steel and flint from him, and within seconds had a fire crackling to life.

"I'm sure it gets easier with practice," Elanor said to Sebastian, trying to comfort him.

He grunted and turned away, hanging his damp cloak over a branch and taking off his boots and setting them near the fire. Everyone else did the same, then huddled close to the warmth of the flames. Fergus lay so close, Elanor was sure she could smell his fur singeing.

Sebastian put his sword over his knees, drying it with a cloth. His red hair flamed in the firelight, his freckles almost exactly the same color.

"All our bread is soaking wet," Quinn said, emptying the contents of her knapsack on the grass.

"Let's use it to make soup," Tom suggested. He took some onions out of the sack, chopped them swiftly, and dropped them in the pot with water, the soggy bread, some sausage, wild garlic and a pinch of salt.

"Isn't it useful having a pot boy on our quest?" Sebastian said in a mocking tone. "He's quite handy with a wooden spoon."

"You don't need to eat any," Tom replied.

Sebastian held up both hands. "Just saying."

"Well, don't," Tom answered, "else you can cook."

"Knights don't cook," Sebastian answered.

"Then knights don't eat," Tom responded, ladling the soup into just three bowls. He handed bowls to the girls, then began to eat his own.

Sebastian jumped up, furious, ready to charge him, but Elanor said pleadingly, "Please don't fight."

"Is it my fault the pot boy can't take a joke?" Sebastian muttered.

"Maybe, if your jokes were funny—" Tom said.

Sebastian was charging forward again, fists clenched, when the unicorn suddenly lunged forward and pressed the point of his horn to Sebastian's heart. The boy stopped, all his freckles standing out as his face went white.

For a moment all was still, then the unicorn turned

his head and looked at Tom. Nobody moved or spoke.

The unicorn bowed his head and stepped back into the shadows, almost invisible in the tangle of thorn.

Shakily, Tom ladled a bowl of soup for Sebastian and they both sat down. Through the silence, the group stared at the unicorn.

"He needs a name," Quinn said, after a moment.

If they hadn't known he was there, Elanor thought, they might have walked right past him. He was perfectly camouflaged. "What did you say Arwen called the hawthorn tree?" Elanor asked Quinn.

"Whitethorn," Quinn answered.

"No, the other name."

"Quickthorn?"

"Yes. Quickthorn. That would be a good name for him. He's so quick and strong and full of life, and his horn is as sharp as those thorns."

The unicorn gave a soft whicker.

"See? He likes it. That's his name. Quickthorn." Elanor realized she was smiling. Looking around the campfire, she saw gladly that everyone else was smiling too.

5

THE OAK KING

"What shall we do now?" Elanor asked.

"We need a plan," Tom said. "We can't keep just wandering in the forest, hoping we stumble upon a griffin."

"Or a dragon," Sebastian said.

A strange look came over Quinn's face, as if she was listening to something the others couldn't hear. "We need to head east," she said. "The griffin can be found to the east."

"How do you know that?" Tom demanded.

She flushed and one hand went up to hold the wooden talisman she wore around her neck. "Um . . . I . . . I just know."

"How?" he asked again.

Quinn's color deepened. Again she touched the wooden talisman. It was intricately carved into an old man's face, his hair and beard like leaves. "You know how Arwen gave me this medallion, just before we fled the castle?"

Elanor nodded, touching the silvery blue moonstone ring that had been the Grand Teller's gift to her. Called the Traveler's Stone, it shone out in the darkness and showed the path ahead.

"Well, it . . . talks to me sometimes." Quinn looked defiant, as if expecting no one to believe her.

"*Talks* to you?" Sebastian cried, but more in amazement than disbelief.

"Not often. But he spoke to me just then."

"So he told you to go east?" Tom asked.

Quinn nodded. "He said that the king of birds and beasts dwells high on a crag to the east. I think he means the griffin. A griffin's meant to have the hindquarters and tail of a lion, which is the king of the beasts, and the head and forequarters of an eagle, which is the king of the birds."

"So he says there's a griffin in this forest?" Tom asked, getting excited. "What else does he say?"

Quinn looked embarrassed, and dropped her hand from the wooden face. "He says to stop grabbing at him, he can't see with my hand over his eyes."

Elanor, Tom and Sebastian stared at the wooden face in wonderment. The wooden face stared back.

"Now he says you all look like baby birds with your goggling eyes and gaping mouths."

The other three shut their mouths at once.

"How can he talk?" Elanor ventured after a while. "Is he alive?"

To her amazement, the carved wooden mouth of the medallion began to move. His leafy eyebrows rose high and then dropped. Quinn began to speak, slowly, with many pauses as she stopped to listen.

"He is the Oak King, he says, carved many hundreds of years ago by a hand long dead. Long ago, longer than we can measure, an acorn fell to the ground, cracked open, and a green sprout unfurled. It rooted in the dark earth, and unfolded a leaf. The sprout grew and grew until it was a tree, laden with leaves and new acorns of its own. It grew till its green crown hid the sun, and its roots probed the hidden shadows of the earth's heart. Lightning shattered its trunk, and it fell. The bog sucked it down, and for a long time it was lost. But what goes into the bog must, in the end, come out."

Quinn's voice was quiet, awed, and the others listened in silence.

"He was found and created, and has been worn at the throat of many a witch. He was young when the world was young, and now he is old."

For a moment, the wooden face fell still, and the eyes seemed to look inward. Then he began to speak again, the leafy fronds of his hair and beard flowing as his mouth moved.

Quinn continued slowly. "He says he is the heat in our hearth, the shade that shields us from the sun, the beam that holds up our house, the board of our table, the handle of our hoe, the door of our home. Of him was our cradle made . . . and so too shall be our coffin."

There was a long silence. Fergus whined and shifted closer to Tom, leaning his head on the boy's shoulder.

"Does he have a name?" Tom wanted to know at last, unusually subdued.

"He says he has many names. Some have called him Green George, others Jack-in-the-Green, others the Oak King. Some have called him Sylvan Adam."

Again there was a long silence. Then the wooden mouth spoke again, and Elanor felt she could almost read his lips and understand.

"He says we can call him Sylvan," Quinn said.

"Ask him . . . ask Sylvan . . . how we're to catch the griffin," Tom said.

Ask me yourself, little man . . . Elanor could have sworn she heard the words, but decided that it must have been the rustle of the wind in the thorn trees.

"He says to ask him yourself," Quinn said.

"So, sir . . . Sylvan . . . how do we catch the griffin?" Tom asked awkwardly.

The wooden mouth moved in answer.

Quinn frowned, looking puzzled. "I don't know what his answer means. It's some kind of riddle."

"I thought you were the riddle master," Sebastian said. "Surely you can work it out."

"I'll have to think about it," she said, before slowly repeating the verse.

"*At the sound of me, women may dance*
Or sometimes weep.
At the sound of me, men may dream
Or stamp their feet.
At the sound of me, babes may laugh
Or drift to sleep.
At the sound of me, beasts may come
and their master greet."

"I don't get it," Tom said.

"No, me neither," Quinn admitted. "We need time to work it out . . . The answer will come, in time."

Elanor sighed. She was sure her governess, Mistress Mauldred, would not approve of such cryptic riddles. *A lady must always endeavor to be sweet and simple.*

Sweet and simple? How was one to awaken the sleeping heroes and save Wolfhaven while being sweet and simple? For the first time, Elanor thought that perhaps her governess was a fool.

"What about the dragon?" Sebastian demanded. "Ask him about that."

"Ask him where the bog-men come from," Tom interrupted. "Are they still hunting us? And why is Lord Mortlake doing this? Does he really want to kill us?"

"My father? How is my father? Is he hurt?" Elanor's words suddenly burst out and tumbled over the top of each other. "What have they done to him? What about all the people of Wolfhaven?"

"What about my mam?" Tom wanted to know. "Is she safe?"

"Have we been sent on a wild-goose chase?" Sebastian asked. "Should we be trying to get help, rather than continuing on this quest?"

Elanor had so many questions she hardly knew where to start. "Is there really a griffin in this forest? Won't it be wild and savage? How can we tame it?"

The mouth spoke, the eyes wild and rolling in the wooden face.

Quinn held up one hand against them. "He says *too many questions!*" Then, after a pause, Quinn added, "He says he is very old and tired, and needs to rest."

With that, the wooden eyes slowly closed.

NIGHT IN THE WITCHWOOD

E lanor huddled into her shawl, too tired to sleep. Her whole world was topsy-turvy and she didn't know how to turn it the right way again. Darkness had fallen, but no stars could be seen through the canopy of the forest. Strange loud noises began, booming through the darkness. Elanor shrank back.

"It's just a toad," Quinn said, leaning forward to throw another branch on the fire. Fergus put his head on Elanor's lap and she rubbed his soft ears, comforted.

"We'd better take turns to keep watch," Tom said.

"Great idea," said Sebastian. "You're up first." He rolled over, huddling his knees under his velvet jerkin.

Tom grunted, wrapped himself in his cloak, then

rummaged through his knapsack, bringing out his spare bowstrings to dry by the fire. He found the wooden flute Arwen had given him at the bottom of the bag.

By the light of the flickering flames, Elanor saw that the flute had been carved in the primitive shape of a bird. It had a small round head and a pointed beak, and the elongated shape of wings bending backward. The wood was knotted and crooked, with six holes above, and one below.

Tom blew into the flute. It made no sound at first, and then suddenly it screeched. Fergus shifted restlessly.

Tom tried again, but only to make more screeching. This time, the wolfhound howled.

"Shhh, Fergus," Tom said, and tried once more. A few notes came out, followed by another hair-raising screech.

Fergus howled again, louder this time, and he was answered by distant howls from the forest.

Everyone froze. It was an eerie sound that echoed around them.

At last the howls died away.

Tom looked down at the flute in his hand, then flung it away in frustration. It thumped against a hawthorn tree, then fell into the shadows.

"You shouldn't throw the Grand Teller's gift away so lightly, Tom," Quinn's voice said from the darkness. "It'll be important somehow. You'll see."

"It's useless," Tom answered unhappily.

"Arwen said it was made of wood from the elder tree," Quinn said. "It's a very magical tree, Tom."

"You think all trees are magical," Sebastian jeered.

"Yes," she agreed and turned back to Tom, "and I've heard that flutes made from elder can call the spirits of the forest to them."

Tom grunted impatiently, leapt up, and strode across the clearing. He groped under the razor-sharp thorn trees, muttering under his breath.

"Happy?" he demanded, coming back into the light of the fire, the flute in his scratched hands.

"Yes," Quinn replied.

Elanor listened to the sound of Tom blowing into the flute, experimenting, moving his fingers.

Sometimes the flute made no sound at all, sometimes it squawked, and, once or twice, it blew a note of surprising sweetness. Elanor rested her cheek on her hand, certain that she could never sleep. She thought about her father. Where was he? Was he hurt? Was he worried about her?

If my father dies, I will be the Lady of Wolfhaven Castle, Elanor suddenly realized. It was a terrifying thought that made her shudder. She was only twelve years old, far too young to rule over the castle and its fields and forests . . .

Then she had an even more terrifying thought. *Would there be anyone left to lead?*

Tears wet her cheeks. *I have to rescue my father. I have to wake the sleeping heroes and make the prophecy come true!*

A long time later, Elanor felt a hand on her shoulder, shaking her awake. It was Sebastian, and the sky behind him was streaked with rose. She'd slept, even though it felt like she'd lain awake all night, worrying.

"Your turn to stand watch," he said, yawning, then rolled himself in his cloak to sleep.

Elanor sat, wrapped in her shawl, all her trust in Fergus who snored noisily nearby. The unicorn stood among the thorn trees, one leg relaxed. He raised his horned head and looked at her, and gave a soft whicker. She smiled at him and rose to her feet, stepping over her sleeping friends to stand beside him, stroking his satiny neck, leaning her face into his mane.

It was eerie being the only one awake in the dark forest. She looked up through the dark canopy of shifting leaves. A blackbird began to sing, and she thought again of her father. With all her heart, she hoped he was unhurt. *I'm alive*, she thought, trying to send him a silent message. *We're doing our best to save you. We'll find the griffin and the dragon and sea serpent too, and we'll raise the sleeping warriors. Have faith in us.*

She stroked the silver-brown flank of the unicorn, and felt the subtle shift of muscles under the smooth skin. *Be brave,* she told herself. *Be strong.*

When it was almost light, Elanor woke the others and they were soon packed up and on their way, heading east. It was hard to set their course by the sun under the heavy canopy of trees. Paths did not always run the way they wanted. Again and again the group had to stop and worry and argue, before at last finding a way forward.

Elanor was riding the unicorn, hands clenched on the reins, when she heard a sudden whirr. A huge, iridescent beetle whizzed past.

"Look!" she said to Sebastian, who rode behind her. "Did you see that?"

Another zoomed past, as bright as a flaming arrow. It was so close, its wings grazed her cheek. Elanor couldn't help flinching.

Another buzzed past, and another.

"Look!" Elanor said again. She pointed in utter amazement. Crouched on the back of the beetle was a tiny, scowling winged creature. It wore a beetle carapace as armor, and a beetle's skull as a helmet. In one hand it carried a hard and shiny whip, like a claw. In the other was a thin, brown stalk. Elanor watched, paralyzed with surprise, as the tiny creature lifted the stalk to its mouth and spat into it.

Elanor cried out as she was pricked in the side of her neck. She clapped one hand to the sting. Dimly she heard Sebastian cry out, and then Quinn. Fergus the wolfhound yelped. Again and again she was stung with tiny, whirring darts.

Elanor had no time to do more than scream. The world whirled around her. She tried to grab the unicorn's mane, but it slipped through her fingers. She felt herself falling, falling, falling. Then the ground leapt up towards her.

7

→→ THE HAG →→

Sebastian groaned and put one hand to his aching head. He tried to open his eyes, but the light was as sharp as a lance. He rolled his head away from it.

Somebody seized him under the armpits and dragged him, slowly and painfully, over hard, knobbly roots. Sebastian groaned and tried to wrest himself free, but he didn't have the strength. He pried open his eyes and saw the most hideous face hanging above him. Gaunt and bony, furrowed with deep lines, with strange milky-white eyes and a sunken mouth, all surrounded by straggling gray hair.

Sebastian flinched. The grip under his arms was sharp and strong; he couldn't jerk free. He was hauled up and through a narrow opening, bumped and bruised on all sides. Shadows fell on his face, and he dropped heavily into crackling leaves. Instinctively he curled on his side, his head swimming and his stomach churning.

A cool damp cloth was laid on his head, covering his eyes. Slowly the wave of dizziness subsided. He managed to sit up, squinting around him.

He was sitting inside the hollow trunk of some great old tree. Green light probed through a narrow slit in the trunk. Sebastian saw Tom sitting next to him, nursing his head in his hands. Fergus sat anxiously beside him, nosing him. Quinn sat up groggily, while Elanor was curled in a ball, moaning.

Sebastian remembered the attack of the giant iridescent beetles and their tiny riders. He put one hand up to the side of his neck and felt a tender welt.

"Ah, you're awake, at last," a creaky voice said.

He looked around and saw the owner of the hideous face. She was an old woman, sitting hunched against the curved wooden wall, matted gray hair hanging in elflocks down her back. Her skin was like dirty scrunched-up parchment. Wrinkles, like crevasses across her forehead, drove down between her straggly gray eyebrows and pinched her withered lips. Her eyeballs were white and blind between heavy bruised-looking lids. She wore an odd collection of dirty old rags, with a grimy knitted hat on her head. Around her neck hung strings of wooden beads, with feathers, shells and seed pods, and a pebble with a spiral engraved upon it. Her back was so hunched and twisted her face was bent down towards her knees.

"Where . . . where are we?" Sebastian croaked. His whole body ached, as if he'd been beaten with clubs, and his heart pumped strangely in his chest.

"You are in my home, the great ash tree called the Nuinn," the old woman said. "My name is Wilda and I am the witch of the Witchwood."

"Greetings, Wilda." Quinn's voice was hoarse and shaky and she looked greenish, but she managed to bow her head formally. "We thank you for your hospitality."

The witch inclined her own gray, matted head in return, regal as any queen. Elanor tried to lift her head to speak, but then moaned and collapsed back on the leaves.

"But how . . . how did we get here?" Sebastian started to get to his feet, but the world swam around him and he staggered and fell back down to his knees. "What's wrong with us?"

"You're feeling the aftereffects of the foxglove," Wilda replied. "It'll make you feel sick and dizzy for a while, and your heart will be unsteady but, never fear, you'll recover."

"Foxglove?" Quinn said, her voice faint.

"Of course," the witch answered.

Quinn stared at her with eyes round with horror. "But foxglove is poisonous."

"Only if you misuse it. Foxglove can be used as a medicine as much as a poison."

"You poisoned us?" Sebastian again tried to get up, but his legs simply folded under him. He felt for his sword, but it was missing from his side.

"Do not fear. Your sword is safely stowed outside the sacred glade," the witch said.

"You had no right to take my sword!"

"I had every right. You may not bring weapons of iron and steel to the Nuinn."

Tom looked urgently for his longbow, and found it leaning against the wall behind him. His quiver was propped next to it, but was empty of its steel-tipped arrows. "Fungus," he gasped, "my arrows!"

Elanor and Quinn quickly realized their dagger sheaths were empty. The only blade that remained was Quinn's small black witch's knife. It hung at her waist as always.

"Your knife is made of black obsidian glass and wood, and so could stay," the witch said, her strange white eyes staring at Quinn. "Do not think of using it as a weapon, though, child. It would not be wise."

After a long pause, Quinn said, "Why are we here? Why did you poison us?"

"It was not I who poisoned you, but the Ellyllon. They dip the tips of thorns in a mixture of the juice from foxglove, skullcap and yellow witcher's herb, and then blow the thorns through the stems of angelica. A simple yet effective weapon for creatures so small."

"But why?" Elanor asked, her narrow face pinched

and white.

"You were riding the unicorn," the witch answered. "You had it bound with leather and chains, and burdened with sacks and bags."

"Quickthorn!" Elanor cried. "Where is he?"

"The unicorn is not far away," the witch answered, turning her blind eyes to Elanor's face. "I'm afraid you will be the one most affected, Lady Elanor, since you were the one who held the unicorn's restraints. The Ellyllon were distressed to see the unicorn bound, and blew many thorns into your flesh."

Elanor was as pale as skim milk. She pressed one hand to her mouth, the other to her heart. Her arms and neck were covered with angry red welts, with one on her cheek causing her lower eyelid to swell.

"The Elly . . . the Elly-what?" Sebastian demanded.

"The Ellyllon, a race of small winged creatures that live here in the forest," the witch answered. "They are fierce, and quick to defend themselves and other creatures from wrongdoing."

"But you don't understand!" Quinn protested. "We *rescued* the unicorn."

"And we needed him to help us carry the bags." Sebastian felt hot and uncomfortable under the witch's unblinking white gaze. "We were being chased . . . we were running as fast as we could . . ."

"He's our friend," Elanor said, clasping both hands together.

"Do you restrain all your friends with ropes?"

Elanor flushed. "Of course not. It wasn't like that. We were afraid he would run away . . . we were being chased, he was frightened . . ."

"And why should the unicorn not flee if he is fearful? Is he not a free creature?"

"Yes, but . . ." Elanor stumbled to a halt, trying to find a way to explain.

"We were trying to keep him safe," Tom said angrily. "Lord Mortlake was going to kill him for his horn. We *saved* him."

"Those leather things attacked us, tried to kill us," Sebastian said.

"Why are you being pursued?" the witch asked. As she spoke, she drew a small stone pot towards her, from a collection tucked in every nook and crevice of the tree's inner trunk. She measured out a spoonful of powder—the color of dried blood—into a wooden cup. Then she measured out dried leaves and flower buds from the many small pouches that hung from her woven belt, dropping them into a heavy stone mortar. She ground the herbs with a pestle, put them in the cup, and added steaming water from a clay kettle. She sniffed it, added a spoonful of honey, then passed the cup to Elanor. When the girl hesitated, the witch smiled, showing a few crooked stumps of teeth. "Do not fear, Lady Elanor, it'll make you feel much better."

"How do you know who I am?" Elanor whispered.

"I am the witch of the Witchwood, I always know who . . . or what . . . trespasses in my domain."

"Then you must already know about the bog-men," Tom said.

She hesitated. "Those poor lost souls, raised out of the bog by the oldest and blackest of magic?"

There was a surprised silence. The group had heard Lord Mortlake call the pungent leathery creatures his bog-men, but they did not realize they'd been raised from the muddy swamps.

"They want to catch us and drag us back," Elanor said, draining the cup. Slowly color returned to her cheeks. "If you know that I am Elanor de Belleterre, daughter of the Lord of Wolfhaven, then you must know also that our castle has fallen to Lord Mortlake, who attacked in the dead of night with an army of soldiers and those bog-men."

"No, I did not know," the witch replied. "Wolfhaven Castle lies outside my forest's boundaries. All I knew was that an unnatural mist had rolled from the north, tainted with dark magic, and that much blood had been spilled, causing the creatures of the field and the farrow to bolt for cover in my domain."

"It was Lord Mortlake who raised that mist," Elanor said. "We escaped, thinking we'd left him behind, but then the bog-men . . . they must've picked up our trail. They would've killed us, but Quickthorn saved us."

"He stabbed them all straight through the heart," Sebastian said with gusto.

"His horn was like a lance of fire," Quinn said. "It smote them dead, turned their flesh to ash and smoke."

That girl reads too many books, Sebastian thought.

Frowning, the witch bent forward and took back the cup from Elanor, washed it out, and made more herbal tea which she passed to Quinn.

"So you have sought shelter in my forest like the creatures of the field and farrow?" she asked.

Tom nodded, hesitating. He flashed a look at the others, silently wondering whether they should tell the witch about the purpose of their journey. Sebastian frowned and shook his head. Elanor, looking anxious, shook her head too.

Quinn scowled at them and nodded her head emphatically. As she began to speak, Sebastian groaned. That girl never listened to anyone!

"There is another reason we're here, Wilda," Quinn said. "You see, Arwen, the Grand Teller of Wolfhaven Castle, sent us on this . . . this quest . . ."

"This *crazy* quest," Sebastian said. "It's nothing but a bag of moonshine, really." He frowned intently at Quinn, willing her to keep her mouth shut, but she hurried on.

"We have to find a unicorn's horn, a dragon's

tooth, a sea serpent scale and a griffin feather," she said. "We have to bring them all together at dawn, to wake the heroes of old, who sleep beneath the castle."

Wilda looked at her in astonishment. "She seeks to wake the sleepers under the castle?" Her voice was filled with horror. "But it's been so long. Is it possible?"

"It seems *impossible*," Elanor said. "Except—"

"Except we found a unicorn!" Quinn exulted. "And Sylvan tells us the griffin is here, in this very forest."

"Does he indeed?" the blind witch said, reaching for her staff of carved white wood and hauling herself to her feet. "Then I hope he can tell you where. For I know every hidden path and secret way through these woods, and have traveled them all my life, yet I have never seen claw nor feather of this griffin. Trust me. I have searched for it many years now. I would give anything to have found it. There is no griffin in this forest."

8

THE WITCH'S FRIENDS

Q uinn scrambled to her feet and followed the witch through the narrow rift in the tree trunk. The movement made her head swim and her heart lurch. She had to stand still for a moment, eyes filled with swirling stars, before the dizziness passed.

The sun was sinking in the west. It slanted through the trees, illuminating the small grove that lay before the giant ash tree. It was perfectly round, with smooth turf starred with white clover. Quinn recognized apple, hazel, hawthorn, oak and elder growing close around the grove, all sacred to witches, and—growing wild in the verges—carrot, angelica, burdock, sorrel and other useful herbs and vegetables.

In the center of the grove was a fireplace of river stones, with a small fire, hazing the air with blue smoke. Wilda was crouched before it, feeding it twigs and handfuls of dried moss.

Not all witches are wise, little maid, Sylvan said quietly in her mind. *Not all hags are honorable.*

Quinn felt a twinge of doubt. *We need to find the griffin,* she told Sylvan. *This old witch could help us.*

Or hinder you, the Oak King returned. She felt the talisman warm against her skin and put one hand up to touch it.

I have to try, she told him firmly. *Arwen sent us on this quest. I cannot fail her.*

The thought of the Grand Teller brought a sting of tears to her eyes. Quinn was a foundling, an abandoned baby, with no parents of her own. The old castle witch had taken her in and taught her the Ways of the Wise. Arwen had cared for Quinn, teaching her to read, and calculate in her head, and to know the names and properties of plants, stones, seeds and stars. Quinn loved her with all her heart and trusted her with her own life. She didn't even know if Arwen had survived the attack on the castle . . .

A soft whicker drew her attention. Quickthorn was standing knee-deep in wild flowers, head held high, looking at her with dark eyes. The sight of the unicorn gave Quinn courage. They had found one beast. They would find the other three.

"Please, Wilda," she said, "surely you can help us? We have so little time. Our friends are in the hands of our enemy. We need to save them!"

"Please?" Elanor pleaded. Quinn turned and saw that her friends had all crawled out of the rift in the ash tree. They looked dirty and disheveled, with red welts on their faces and necks from the poison darts. Sebastian's face was surly and suspicious, and he gripped his belt where his sword normally hung. Tom was alert and curious, his eyes examining every detail of the landscape before him. He carried his longbow and empty quiver over one shoulder, while one hand rested on his wolfhound.

"If you can't help us, we need to be on our way," he said. "Where are our weapons and our packs?"

"It is almost twilight," the witch said, twisting

her face around to see them. "It would be foolish to blunder off into the forest now. You'll only get lost."

"We'll be fine." Sebastian folded his arms, scowling at the witch. "Now where's my sword?"

"We have a compass," Tom said. "We know we have to travel east. There's still some light left. We can make up some ground before it's fully dark."

"I'm about to cook supper," the witch said. "Aren't you hungry?"

The boys hesitated. They were always hungry. Quinn herself didn't feel much like eating. She still felt dizzy and sick, and her heart was thumping hard.

"We have food in our packs," Tom said. "But thank you for the offer."

"Besides," Sebastian said, "you said you can't help us."

"Believe me, I would help if I could," the witch said. She waved her hand towards the fire. "Come, sit down, rest yourselves. The poison will take some time to work its way out of your systems. Please, come and eat with me, and I'll tell you what little I know."

She's lonely, Quinn thought. *She just wants our company.* She went and sat down cross-legged on the grass. With a jerk of her head, she told the others to join her. Slowly they came and sat down too, Fergus lying close to his master, his head resting on his paws.

The old woman lifted a large clay pot onto the fire, settling it into the hot coals, then reached out blindly with her hands, patting the grass until she found a wicker basket. She drew it towards her and lifted out mushrooms and some muddy plant roots. She began to peel the roots with her small black witch's knife.

"I too have been searching for the griffin," she admitted. "They say that one of its feathers can cure blindness. I have searched for many years."

"But you're blind," Sebastian blurted out. "You couldn't see it even if it was sitting in a tree right above your head."

The witch turned her cloudy-white eyes towards Sebastian. His cheeks began to redden. "There are many ways to see," she said. "And I have not always been blind. It came upon me slowly. When I realized that I would no longer be able to see the hares leap in the meadows in spring, or the autumn turn the leaves to flame, I wept many tears."

The witch sat quietly, slowly peeling away the muddy skin of the root to show pure yellow flesh, which she then chopped into the clay pot. She fumbled for her wooden spoon and stirred the stew, all her movements slow and painful. Quinn's heart swelled with pity for her. She wondered how the old woman managed alone in the forest, blind and crippled.

It was growing dark. Bats flitted through the sky, and a few stars shone out above the dark shapes of the trees. Then Quinn heard a shrill bark from the twilight. Fergus's head came up and his ears pricked forward. He growled and rose to his feet, all the hair along his spine stiffening. The bark came again, then the gekkering sound of fox cubs playing. The wolfhound's body elongated into a hunting pose, one paw lifted, his nose stretched out.

Quinn seized his ruff, holding him still. Tom began to protest, but she shushed him with a finger to her lips.

A red fox came slinking out of the forest, its throat and chest a triangle of white. It gazed at the children warily and gave a little warning growl, then crept up to the old witch, nestling against her. Behind the vixen bounded two fox cubs, knocking each other over clumsily. Quinn watched, entranced. A smile crept over Elanor's pale face.

Then a squirrel came scampering down a tree, its paws full of hazelnuts. It leapt up to the old woman's shoulder and she took the nuts and put them in another clay pot to roast on the fire, then petted the squirrel in thanks. The fox looked up, but made no other move. Fergus, however, barked and bounded forward.

The witch turned and held up one gnarled hand. "Halt," she said. Fergus skidded to a stop, and sat with a plop only inches from the old woman. She reached out and rubbed his head between the ears. "Good boy."

Fergus wagged his tail and put out his nose to smell the fox. The fox, unafraid, touched his nose with hers.

The witch had friends, Quinn realized.

"I may be blind, but I have many friends in the forest," the witch said, echoing Quinn's thought eerily. "They have eyes, ears and noses much more acute than yours, and they too have seen no sign of any griffin."

9

THE
WOODEN FLUTE

"But the Witchwood spreads for miles and miles," Tom said. "How can you know everything that lives within?"

"I was born here," the witch said. "I have traveled every path and explored every valley, both before and after I lost my sight. If a griffin lived here, I would know."

"Yet you say you've searched for it yourself, Wilda," Quinn said. "Surely you wouldn't do so if you didn't believe it existed?"

The old witch sighed. "I hoped the old tales were true. I hoped I could find a griffin and tame him and ask him to surrender a feather to me. I *so* longed to have my sight back again. But it was a foolish dream."

"Sylvan says the king of birds and beasts dwells high on a crag to the east," Quinn said. "Surely that means the griffin?"

"I don't know," Wilda replied, shifting her rags. "Maybe the griffin lived there once upon a time . . ."

Quinn lifted the wooden medallion in her hand and stared down at it, scowling in concentration. The wooden eyes looked up into hers, the wooden mouth moved. After a moment, her face cleared. She looked up at the witch. "See?"

"I do see," Wilda answered slowly. Her face had changed, the deep grooves around her mouth and eyes lessening.

"Did Sylvan speak?" Elanor asked.

"What did he say?" Sebastian demanded.

"Did he say the griffin exists?" Tom wanted to know.

"He said there is a gateway far to the east, where the sun rises between its pillars on the midsummer morn. If we dare to travel through we will find ourselves on the shore of a hidden lake. *Follow the pathway of gold, and we shall find the king of birds and beasts, high on his eyrie near the hole to the sky.*" Quinn's eyes were bright and eager.

"He can never say anything straight, can he?" Sebastian said.

Quinn shot him an angry look. "You should be more respectful. The Oak King is very old and wise. He's our only hope of finding the griffin right now."

"Sorry," Sebastian mumbled.

"So you heard him too, Wilda?" Elanor asked.

"Indeed. You could hear him too, Lady Elanor, if you listened more deeply."

"So do you know this place . . . this gateway?" Tom asked the witch.

"I know the gateway of stones. It is forbidden to pass through. My mother always made me promise I would never set foot there. She said those who go through never come back."

"Great," Tom said.

"Oh well. No valor without risk, no glory without danger." Sebastian rubbed the amber of his brooch, a habit Tom had seen him do many times since the

Grand Teller had given it to him.

"I would like to feel that brooch," the witch said unexpectedly, turning to him.

Sebastian stared at her in surprise. Reluctantly he unpinned the brooch and passed it to her. It was made of warm rowan wood, carved in the shape of a dragon coiled around a smooth oval of amber. Wilda rubbed her fingertips over the serrated ends of the wings, the coil of the tail, then lifted it to her nose, sniffing. Then she held it out to the fire, squinting as though she could see the golden glow of the flames through the amber.

"A strange gift for a boy like you," Wilda said. "Arwen must see something in you that I do not."

"It's not a strange gift," Sebastian protested. "She knew my family's badge is a dragon."

"Maybe that is reason enough. Certainly she had some reason to give such powerful gifts to children."

Sebastian took the brooch back from her. "So it *is* powerful? What does it do?"

"Its power will reveal itself in time, if it is ready," she answered cryptically.

Sebastian stared down at the brooch, then held it to the fire. The amber glowed brightly. "Maybe it conjures fire," he said hopefully, then looked up in indignation when the witch gave a harsh bark of laughter.

The fox cubs bounded closer, yipping in loud amusement. "Maybe indeed," said Wilda.

"It's unfair," Tom said. "Elanor got a ring that lights up the way, Quinn got a wise old talking head, Sebastian got a brooch that can maybe conjure fire, and all I got is an old whistle."

"Is that so, Tom Pippin?" The witch held out her hand to Tom. "May I see it?"

"It doesn't work," said Tom, digging it out of his pocket and giving it to her.

Wilda ran her fingers over the flute, feeling the shape of the carved bird, and the holes carved along its length. She smelled it and, rather oddly, tasted it with the tip of her tongue. Then she began to play it.

Haunting music lilted into the twilight air. The fox cubs stopped playing and sat down to listen, heads tilted curiously. The unicorn stopped cropping grass and lifted his head. The forest seemed to still, all the birdsong stopped. Shivers ran up and down Tom's body. He'd never heard such a lonely, but beautiful, sound. Each note was pure and perfect.

The squirrel crept closer, one paw resting on the witch's tattered skirt. A hare loped through the wild flowers, then sat, long ears upright. Then, magically, a roe deer stepped delicately out from the forest, a fawn close by its side.

The song came to an end, and the witch lowered the flute. There was a long silence.

"Can you teach me to do that?" Tom asked at last, his face alight with eagerness.

"In the morning, perhaps," the witch answered. "Let us eat first, and rest. For the foxglove poison takes more than just a few hours to leave your blood."

Surprisingly, the witch's stew was almost as good as his mother's. Tom couldn't eat more than a mouthful, though. He kept worrying whether his mother had anything to eat. Was she hurt or afraid?

He wished he didn't feel so sick. He wanted to be on his way, doing something—anything—to rescue his mother and the people of Wolfhaven. Glancing around, he saw that the others weren't eating either.

The witch laid down her spoon. "You must eat. You need to regain your strength."

Sebastian obediently ate a few mouthfuls, but Quinn said, "I'm sorry. I can't."

The witch looked from one face to another and said, "Would you all feel better if you knew how your families were? If you could see them with your own eyes?"

"Of course," said Elanor. The others nodded.

The witch sighed. "Quinn, go into the ash tree and bring me my obsidian ball and my bags of herbs."

"Angelica and hawthorn?" Quinn asked.

The witch shook her head. "No. Mugwort, wormwood and adder's tongue."

Quinn frowned. "But . . . they're poisonous . . . and only used in black magic . . ."

"It is black magic we need tonight," the witch answered.

BLACK MAGIC

Tom desperately wanted to see his mother and know that she was alive, but he was wary of this hunch-backed old witch with her eerie white eyes. Looking around the fire, he could see Elanor and Sebastian both looked tense and frightened, but neither made any protest. Hope won out over all their fear.

Quinn returned, a small black ball held carefully between her hands, several pouches of herbs dangling from her wrist. The witch threw a few handfuls of herbs onto the fire, and a bitter-smelling smoke billowed out. It made Tom cough, and his eyes water.

"Look into the ball," the witch said and the four children obeyed. Tom could see the tiny reflection of the flickering flames and his own face, weirdly distorted. "Gaze into your eyes."

Tom gazed. His eyes were like black holes.

The witch began to chant:

"Blazing fire shining bright,

Give us now the second sight,

Let us see with your clear light,

Part the veils of the night."

Tom blinked and his vision swam. He felt strangely dizzy. He tried to focus on his reflection in the obsidian ball, but the flames were twisting and changing their shape. He leaned closer. The flames looked like the dark shapes of men and women, hunched together in a dark cell. A lantern hung above their heads.

"Fire crackling loud and clear,

Part the folds of our ear,

Let us listen without fear,

Give us all there is to hear."

Tom heard a low murmur of voices. "What will they do to us?" a frightened woman's voice said.

"We have to try to escape," a man said. Tom recognized the voice of Sir Kevyn, Wolfhaven Castle's master-of-arms.

"But there are too many of them!" another man protested. The vision was becoming clearer. Tom saw the speaker was Algernon the butler.

"We must try," Lord Wolfgang said. He was sitting upright, his face looking haggard and exhausted, but full of resolution. "I refuse to spend the rest of my life locked up in a dungeon."

"They'll kill us if we try to escape," Algernon groaned, wringing his fat hands together. "My lord, you cannot risk it."

"Indeed not," said a familiar voice. Tom gasped as he recognized his mother. Mistress Pippin was kneeling beside Lord Wolfgang, bandaging a wound on his arm with a strip torn from her petticoat. "You just need to be patient, my lord. My boy Tom has gone for help. Don't you fear, he'll not fail us. All we have to do is make sure we stay alive till he gets here."

"He's just a boy! What can he do?" Parker the steward cried.

"He may be just a boy, but he's smart and brave," Mistress Pippin answered. "He'll think of something."

"Don't forget that he's with my apprentice, Quinn," another low voice said, and Tom saw that Arwen lay on a blanket on the ground, her white robe stained with smoke and dirt and blood. Her thin old face was bruised, and her lip swollen and cut, but her eyes were bright with determination. "Lord Sebastian is there too, and your own daughter, Lord Wolfgang. The four of them together will prevail, I am sure of it."

"Quinn!" the steward sneered. "That witch girl's nothing but a barefoot dreamer!"

Arwen lifted herself up on one elbow. "It is often the dreamers of this world who do the most extraordinary things."

"Sebastian is a good boy," Sir Kevyn said. "He won't let us down."

"I've given them all great gifts," Arwen said. "But it is the gifts they carry within them that will see them triumph." She seemed to gaze directly into Tom's eyes as she spoke, and his heart lifted. Could she see them? Did she know they listened from afar?

Mistress Pippin spoke up again. "Quinn may be a dreamer, but I've never known a brighter spirit.

They'll come up with a plan. And, my lord . . ." She hesitated.

"Yes, Mistress Pippin?" Lord Wolfgang sounded weary.

"Your lass will never rest till she has you back safe again, of that you can also be sure."

Lord Wolfgang dropped his head into his hands. "If I could only know that she was alive . . . unhurt . . . I cannot bear to think of her alone and frightened."

"She's not alone," Mistress Pippin comforted him. "She's with Tom, Quinn and Lord Sebastian, and with my boy's wolfhound too. Fergus is a faithful old dog, he'll guard them with his life."

Tom heard a soft thump as the wolfhound's tail beat against the ground. He couldn't tear his gaze away from the obsidian ball, however. He wanted desperately to speak to his mother, to assure her that he was doing his best to save them.

"Leaping fire as you dance,

Let us share a secret glance,

Give us now one last chance,

Join our minds in fire's trance," the old witch chanted.

Tom saw the lantern in the vision swaying, sending shadows leaping over the prisoners.

Mistress Pippin glanced up in irritation. Suddenly her eyes widened. She stared into the hissing flame. "Tom?" she faltered.

"I'm here," Tom shouted. "Mam, I'm coming! I'm coming to get you!"

He was vaguely aware of all the others calling out too. In the vision, Lord Wolfgang had started to his feet, both hands held out. Arwen was struggling to rise, her eyes blazing with excitement. "Quinn?" she called. "Is it you? Quinn?"

The vision blurred and faded away.

Tom found himself standing by the fire, his eyes stinging from the smoke, his voice hoarse and broken. He dashed his hand over his eyes and saw Elanor kneeling nearby, both hands desperately stretched out to the ball, and Quinn calling to Arwen, tears on her face.

Sebastian, however, sat hunched and turned away.

Quinn knelt beside him. "Sebastian, what is it? What's wrong?"

He jerked a shoulder. "Nothing."

"But didn't you see? They're all alive," Quinn's voice trailed away as Sebastian looked at her in astonishment.

"Yes. I saw them all. My father, my mother, my sisters. They were laughing and playing games together. They don't care at all."

There was a long silence. Tom slowly realized that Sebastian had seen a different vision to him and the girls. Sebastian had seen his own family.

"They mustn't know," Quinn said.

Sebastian turned to stare at her. "Do you think so?" he asked in a very different voice. "Really?"

"If everyone was taken prisoner, how was word to get out?" Elanor asked.

"It's only been a few days since Wolfhaven Castle was attacked," Tom reminded him.

"Maybe nobody knows," Elanor added.

Sebastian shrugged. "You'd think they'd *feel* something. I mean, here I am . . ." He gestured down at his torn and filthy jacket, his arm bound up with a bloody rag. "We've been fighting for our lives!"

Tom nodded, understanding something of what Sebastian felt. It must have been awful to see his family laughing, heedless of the danger Sebastian was in. The vision Tom had seen had been a great comfort, and must have been to Elanor and Quinn too. They had seen the ones they loved the most, bruised and afraid, but alive.

Sebastian stood up, unsteadily. "I have to get a message to them. Father could send troops, he could come himself and help. I should have ridden for him straightaway. He'll think I'm a fool." He kicked at a stick and sent it tumbling away, through the smoke, into the darkness.

Suddenly the witch spoke. "Tomorrow," she said. "I will send birds with messages. For now, you must rest. I have to warn you that your sleep will be disturbed tonight. The night hag shall ride you. Try not to believe what you see."

THE BOOK OF STORIES

The night was a chain of nightmares, each worse than the one before.

Tom was relieved when morning came and he could get up and stagger, stiff legged and crusty eyed, to the stream to wash his face and have a drink.

Elanor was white-faced and red eyed, Quinn silent and troubled. Sebastian was surly and aggressive. "You said I could send a message to my father," he said to the witch, as soon as he was on his feet. "How? I want to do it now."

"I need paper," the witch said. "And ink and a quill. Quinn, in the tree is an old book. Tear me out the end pages. Tom, gather me charcoal from the fire and mix it with a little water. Elanor, check the plum trees and see if any are oozing gum. Sebastian, if I call down a crow, can you seize a couple of its wing feathers?"

They all did what they were told, Sebastian having the hardest job and earning himself a sharp peck on his hand from the crow. They mixed the charcoal with the gum and a little water, and Quinn carefully cut the feathers to make quill pens. Elanor tore the pages into strips, then Quinn wrote a message on each strip of paper: *Wolfhaven fallen. Need help urgently.*

Tom rolled each strip as tightly as he could, and then secured it with a tiny blob of softened gum. The witch called down a dozen birds and the notes were attached to their legs with string and more gum.

"How will we know if the messages get through?" Sebastian asked.

The witch shrugged. "At least you will have tried."

Sebastian made an impatient movement. "I should head south, I should make sure my father knows."

Quinn seized his hand. "Sebastian, please. We need to stick together. Arwen sent us on this quest for a reason. We have to trust her."

"Please," Elanor added imploringly.

"You're not strong enough to journey on today," the witch said. "You must rest and recover."

"But surely the foxglove poison would have passed by now?" said Tom.

"That is true," said Wilda. "But the smoke last night—"

"That smoke last night was poisonous, too?" Sebastian interrupted. "You did this to us?"

"There is always a cost," she answered.

Sebastian glared at her, but he was clearly feeling unsteady. The girls were able to persuade him, eventually, to sit down and eat and rest awhile.

Meanwhile, Wilda showed Tom how to play scales on his flute, and demonstrated how he could create different noises by moving his fingers, his tongue, and his breath.

"Keep at it," she told him. "You'll master it in the end."

While Tom careened from screechiness to sweetness, the witch talked with Quinn, showing her many old remedies and spells. She gave her the old book, dusty and tattered. "There are many ancient tales in here," she said. "Perhaps one will tell you where to find the griffin."

Quinn spent the day poring over the brittle, yellowed pages, while Elanor groomed the unicorn till his coat shone like satin. That night, Quinn read them stories of girls turned into owls and boys who fought giants. The old witch listened intently, gnarled hands resting on the red fur of the fox, tears occasionally sliding from her milky eyes.

"I have missed being able to read, almost more than anything else," she said, wiping her eyes.

So Quinn turned the pages, looking for another tale to read out. She found one about a dragon and read it to them eagerly, hoping it might hold some clues to help them on their quest.

There were once a lord and a lady who had a very beautiful daughter. Her name was Tegwen and she put the sun to shame. The lord and his family lived high in the fells, in a castle on the shores of a lake. In the center of the lake was an island and on it grew an ancient rowan tree, guarded by a dragon. Everyone knew the rowan could not be touched without facing the wrath of the mighty beast.

One day, there came a young man to the castle and he saw Tegwen and fell in love with her. He asked for her hand in marriage, and Tegwen was more than willing, for she too had fallen in love with him. Her father sneered at him though, and said that he was not fit to wed his daughter. "Tegwen must marry a brave and mighty warrior," her father said.

"I am brave and strong," the young man said, "and I love her. I will always protect her."

"Prove it," said the lord.

"How? I'll do anything," the young man declared.

The lord told the young man that he must bring Tegwen the berries of the rowan tree. So the young man swam the lake and stole a handful of berries. The father said it was not enough. He must steal a whole branch. So the young man swam the lake again and cut a thick branch from the tree, heavily laden with berries. Again the lord said it was not enough. He told the young man he must find the dragon's own egg, kept buried under the rowan tree's roots.

So the young man swam again to the island and seized hold

of the rowan tree and shook it until, at last, he'd wrested it from the ground. There, nestled in the tree's torn roots, was the dragon egg, glowing with light. The young man seized it and turned to run, but it was too late. The dragon fell upon him.

All day they fought, and all night, and all the next day. At last, the young man felled the dragon, severing its head from its body. Mortally wounded, he managed to swim back to the castle and deliver the dragon's egg into Tegwen's hands before he fell, dead, at her feet.

The blood of the dragon had seeped into the ground, however, opening up a smoking chasm. It split the earth with a great crack and swallowed the castle and the town and the lake, till nothing was left but a treacherous quaking bog. Only Tegwen survived, for she held the dragon's egg in her hands. Weeping, she fled, and for the rest of her days wore the dragon's egg above her heart as a reminder of the brave young man who had died for the love of her.

"Such a stupid girl," Elanor said. "She should have just ignored her father and run away with him."

Tom hid a grin. Elanor was no longer the girl he'd met in her room that day, with *A Lady's Complete*

Guide to Manners, Morals & Modesty balanced on top of her head.

"Isn't there a story about the griffin?" he asked Quinn. "We could do with some clues."

Quinn flicked through the pages till she found a story about a griffin. A young man had heard of the griffin that lived in the heart of the forest, guarding a hoard of gold, she told them. He had set out to find it, but never returned. His brother went in search of him and also failed to return. So the youngest brother went after them and found the griffin. Instead of trying to steal the monster's gold, however, he helped him by drawing a thorn out of his paw. The griffin, in thanks, gave him as much gold as he could carry and so he returned home, rich and triumphant. Of his brothers, though, nothing was ever found.

The story described the pillars of the stone gateway through which the brothers passed as being "shaped like the head of an eagle and the haunches of a lion."

"That's a clue," Quinn said. "Pillars shaped like a griffin, in the heart of the forest. We just need to keep on looking."

They slept easier that night, and woke feeling stronger the next day. Tom woke first, and reached at once for his flute. He loved moving his fingers, and hearing music spilling like magic into the air. It was as if he had always had some longing inside him, some absence, and the music filled that hole in him.

The others woke and were all keen to finally be on their way.

"I feel almost as strong as ever," Sebastian said, flexing his muscles.

"Stay a while longer," the witch said. "You may feel strong again, but you are still affected. One more day should do the trick. Stay. I can teach you things."

But all four shook their heads, so the witch said no more. She went and sat by the fire, her back hunched till it seemed her nose would meet her feet, and played with her necklaces, muttering. Tom and the others packed up their belongings, feeling rather rude and ungrateful for her help.

"I need my sword," Sebastian said.

"And I need my arrows," Tom added.

They both looked at the muttering witch and hesitated.

Elanor suddenly screamed. Both boys spun around to her. She was running towards the ash tree and behind her was a dark whirling storm of flying beetles. The sun glinted on their iridescent wings and on the helmets of the tiny Ellyllon that rode their backs.

"Run!" Tom shouted. "Quinn! It's those beetle riders again. Get under cover!"

Quinn looked up from the book, then shoved it under her arm as she leapt up and ran for the ash tree. In seconds, the beetles were whirring around her head and she cried out and tried to bat them away.

Tom ran to her aid, pushing Quinn through the gaping crack in the tree trunk and scrambling in after her. At once, he spun around and peered through the crack, the others jostling to see too. Fergus whined.

The beetles did not attack the ash tree or make any attempt to blow their poison darts through the crack. They whirled past the tree, heading straight to where the old witch was struggling to her feet.

"Wilda!" Quinn gasped.

The witch held out both her arms, and the beetles swarmed all over her. In seconds it looked as if she wore living chain mail, glinting blue and green and golden. Even her face was covered. Then the beetles swarmed up and into the air again, buzzing around her head before zooming away into the forest.

Wilda lifted her straggly gray head and flared her nostrils, breathing in deeply through her nose.

"What's she doing?" Elanor's voice trembled.

"Is she . . . sniffing?" Quinn wondered.

The old witch's blind eyes opened wide in shock. She turned and began to hobble away as fast as she could, the fox streaking ahead of her.

"Something's wrong!" Sebastian said. "Listen to the birds!" A flock of starlings swooped through the air, shrieking a warning.

Tom sniffed the air, then cried out in alarm. "Smoke!"

WILDFIRE

A red wall of fire was racing towards the clearing, billowing with black smoke. It roared like an angry monster, gobbling trees and spitting them out behind as broken, scorched logs and trailing ashes.

"Where's my sword?" Sebastian shouted.

"We can't fight fire with a sword!" Quinn protested.

"I'm not going to try and fight it, I'm not a complete thickhead," he responded, as he gathered up his belongings. "We're going to have to run for it and I'm not leaving without my sword!"

The others joined, swinging their packs over their shoulders and snatching up cloaks and shawls.

"We can't outrun that fire," Elanor said, her face

white with worry. "What should we do?"

"We have to try!" Tom said, grabbing his longbow and the empty quiver. "Hurry!"

"The unicorn needs to come, too," Elanor said, running out into the clearing. "Quickthorn!"

The unicorn reared and whinnied. The witch had a tight hold of his reins, keeping him from bolting, but she was so bent and frail, Sebastian was sure the unicorn would knock her over. He ran to seize the reins from her.

Animals fled from the flames into the clearing, the air ringing with their cries of distress. A squirrel leapt to Wilda's shoulder, and the fox cubs pressed, trembling, against her legs. A stag bolted, followed by a herd of deer, tossing their heads in terror. Weasels and wildcats, bears and badgers, moles and mice, spiders and silverfish, hedgehogs and hornets, all came wriggling or scuttling up to the old witch's feet, scrambling over each other's backs to be as close to her as possible.

The unicorn bucked, fighting to free his head. Sebastian hung on grimly to the reins while the witch hobbled over to her staff and basket.

The air was now thick with smoke. It caught at the back of Sebastian's throat and made him cough. He peered through the haze and saw archers tramping through the forest towards them. They were shooting fiery arrows into the undergrowth, sending flames leaping up, licking the trees and grabbing at vines with greedy hands.

A huge knight wearing a black helmet with boar tusks rode a huge black horse, a sword in his gauntleted hand—Lord Mortlake. Ahead of him ran a black bristled boar, even bigger than the horse, with a massive head and hanging jowls, and drooping, red-rimmed eyes. It had its snout down to the ground, snuffling from side to side. Yellow tusks as long as Sebastian's sword curved out from beside its nose, and thick ropes of drool dragged behind it. As it ran, it snorted and roared, a terrifying noise like a thousand wild pigs set loose.

Lady Mortlake rode the boar's back, her crimson skirt fluttering. "Two bags of gold to the soldier who finds them!" she screeched.

Behind the boar-tusked knight rode a dozen men

in black armor. In the smoke and fiery glare of the flames, the knights were menacing black shadows.

"Lord Mortlake," Quinn whispered. "He's found us. We're doomed!"

Wilda raised high her white staff and brought it down to the ground with a mighty thud. At once there was a flash of lightning, a crack of thunder, and then a deluge of rain. The flames roaring towards the clearing were doused with a hiss and a sizzle.

Wilda thumped the ground with her staff again. At once, all the trees between the clearing and the soldiers began shaking and shuddering. Elanor, Quinn, Tom and Sebastian watched in shock and awe as the trees reached out and wove together their twigs and branches, creating an impenetrable hedge.

Lord Mortlake shouted angrily, and his stallion neighed. Then came the terrifying *chop, chop, chop* of steel against wood.

The old witch beckoned the children urgently. Sebastian hurried towards her, Elanor leading the unicorn, Quinn and Tom close behind. The rain still fell, heavy as water poured from a bucket.

"Boy!" the witch called. "The weapons are hidden behind the apple tree!"

Sebastian ran and seized his sword, buckling it to his belt. He scooped up the daggers and arrows, and ran back to the others who grabbed their weapons from him.

"I won't be able to hold them back much longer," Wilda gasped. She was gripping the staff as if it was the only thing preventing her from falling to the ground. "Come stand before me."

"How do we get away?" Elanor gasped. "We're still too weak—"

"They'll catch us!" Tom looked over his shoulder at the knight battering against the wall of thorns.

"We don't have a hope of escaping!" Quinn gulped.

Chop, chop, crack! The woven trees were buckling under the ax blows.

"They're going to kill us," Elanor said, her voice deadened.

Sebastian said nothing, though his grip on his sword was so tight his knuckles were white.

The witch raised her staff then swiftly brought it

down, banging it sharply on Sebastian's forehead. He cried out and reeled back in pain.

"Quick as a wink, make him shrink!" Wilda cried.

The world spun and tilted. Sebastian felt a weird dizziness. Tingles rushed over his skin. The witch's face grew huge, her body so long she was just a black ragged shape towering over him. He could hear the others shouting and protesting, but the sound was growing strangely far away. Then Sebastian found himself surrounded by lofty blades of grass, taller than his head. Tom's boot was like a mountain!

Gripped with terror, Sebastian reached for his sword. On the grass it seemed merely the size of a needle, his shield as small as a button. Far overhead, a blade bent under the weight of a droplet of water. It fell, crashing down on Sebastian and knocking him to the ground. He scrambled up, drenched and shivering. He couldn't believe the witch could have shrunk him to the size of an ant with no more than a blow of her staff! Bellowing with rage, he ran at her and stabbed her gigantic bare toe with his sword. She shook her foot, knocking him flying.

Tom was dwindling rapidly, and the girls too. In seconds they were all standing beside Sebastian, a tiny wolfhound cowering at Tom's feet.

"Watch out!" Elanor screamed. "Behind you!"

Sebastian spun around.

A giant slug reared over him, its eye-stalks reaching forward. Sebastian lunged forward and would have stabbed it right through its soft, slimy head if an enormous hand had not suddenly reached down from the sky and plucked him up by the back of his jacket.

Sebastian kicked and squirmed and tried to stab the hand with his sword, but he was quickly dropped into a basket. Moments later, Tom and the girls fell on top of him, then Fergus, barking shrilly.

The basket's lid slammed shut.

13

»———→ THE ←———«
SILVER POOL

Banged, bounced, bashed and bruised, the four children—and one small and smelly dog—were thrown from side to side for what seemed like hours.

At first, the inside of the basket was enormous, but slowly it seemed to shrink—or the children seemed to grow—until they were all crammed within it, arms and legs in a tangle.

Elanor was squashed against the lid of the basket. She managed to heave it up with one hand and squirmed around so she could sit up.

"Stop it! You're kicking me in the head," Sebastian protested.

"Sorry!" Elanor peered over the edge of the basket.

The forest blurred past, all green and dark and twisted. Ahead, the proud head of the unicorn and his flowing black mane rose up and down, as he galloped along.

Sebastian pushed, scrambling to get his head free as well. He almost pushed Elanor right out of the basket. "Careful!" she said, grabbing at the edges. "The basket's tied to Quickthorn, and he's running full speed."

Sebastian heaved himself up beside her, ignoring Fergus's yelp. He could hear a strange buzzing sound. "Look! Behind us!"

Elanor looked out. A swarm of beetles chased them, driving the unicorn on faster and faster. Their metallic wings whirred, and the Ellyllon on their back called shrilly, "Ya! Ya!" rattling seed pods with one hand.

Quickthorn's ears were laid back flat, as he leapt fallen logs and swerved around tree roots and boulders at a breakneck speed. Elanor clung on to the basket rim with all her strength.

But she was slowly growing bigger. Soon she and Sebastian had barely enough room to breathe, the basket rim digging into their ribs. Elanor's legs were all tangled up with Quinn's. The witch girl had flung open the other lid of the basket, and she and Tom were jammed together in the opening, while Fergus whined and squirmed beneath them.

Sebastian wrenched himself free, climbing out of the basket and clinging to its side. Tom followed, making more room for the girls.

"Don't fall!" Quinn cried. "You'll be trampled!"

Elanor's arms were aching, but she hung on desperately. The unicorn leapt over a fallen log, and Sebastian was flung off the side of the basket. He landed on Quickthorn's back and slithered down his side towards the ground thundering past below. Elanor and Quinn both screamed and reached for him. One caught his arm, the other his hair. Together they managed to drag him back up.

"That hurt," he said through clenched teeth, his knuckles white as he hung from the side of the basket.

The unicorn began to slow down, tiring, as the ground began to rise.

"Ya! Ya!" The beetles hurtled closer, and one of the Ellyllon spat something through its angelica shooter. Elanor ducked down, but it was just a little dried seed pod, which hit the unicorn on the rump and drove him into a gallop again. Quickthorn swerved, almost sending the children flying, then he leapt over a rock and around a curve in the path.

A wide brown pool lay before them and a waterfall plunged down a cliff, foaming into it and churning its waters. The cliff was so high it was almost impossible to see the cleft from which the waterfall poured.

The path rose steeply. The unicorn galloped up it, skin dark with sweat. Elanor looked backward. The beetles had fallen so far behind that she couldn't see them anymore. There was no sign of Mortlake and his knights, or the giant boar.

She turned back around, but instantly her relief turned to fear. The path was coming to a dead end, far above the pool, and Quickthorn showed no sign of slowing. Instead, he raced towards the edge of the lip and gathered his muscles to jump. Elanor clung on to the basket with all her strength. "Hold on!" she screamed.

The unicorn leapt off the edge of the cliff and soared out over the pool, straight towards the waterfall.

The wild white water crashed down on him and swept over the children. Elanor's fingers were torn from the basket rim. She felt herself dragged out and sucked down towards the maelstrom. She flailed her arms and caught at Quickthorn's mane. Each hair was as thick and wiry as a rope. Elanor clutched it tightly, her body banging painfully against the unicorn's muscled neck. Water crashed over her, and she gulped for air.

The next moment, the unicorn landed inside a dark cave, hooves clattering and skidding on stone. Quickthorn stopped, sides heaving. Elanor lifted herself up, and managed to get one leg astride the unicorn's neck. She looked around as she tried to catch her breath. Ahead was a dark archway, leading deeper into the cave. Behind was a thundering wall of water, allowing just enough light for Elanor to see Quinn's white, frightened face peering out of the basket, beside the miserable snout of a bedraggled wolfhound. Sebastian was crouched on the unicorn's back, gripping the basket's strap.

"Tom!" Quinn gasped. "Where's Tom?"

Elanor looked around. Her heart sank. There was

no sign of him. She pictured Tom being ripped off the unicorn's back by the tumult of the waterfall, falling, falling, falling, down to the wildly churning waters below. Tears began to sting her eyes.

"He'll be fine," Sebastian said roughly. "You can't get rid of a pot boy so easily." He cupped his hands to shout into the cave, his voice weirdly shrill. "Tom!"

"I'm down here," Tom said, in a voice that sounded very small and far away. Elanor looked down and saw Tom hanging on to the end of the unicorn's long mane. Slowly he pulled himself up, hand over hand, and Fergus almost leapt out of the basket in excitement.

"Are you hurt?" Elanor called.

"I'm fine," Tom said, hauling himself up onto the unicorn's back. "Aside from being the size of a bug!"

"I can't believe the unicorn leapt through the waterfall like that!" said Sebastian, his face alight. "I thought we'd all be smashed to pieces on those rocks!"

They all agreed, looking back at the white curtain of water. "But where are we now?" Quinn asked, looking around her at the damp, dark, narrow cave.

"Why did the Ellyllon drive the unicorn on like that?"

"And why did the witch shrink us all down to the size of ants?" Sebastian growled.

"So we could safely escape Lord Mortlake," Quinn replied, wriggling out of the basket so she was no longer squashed up against Fergus, who had now grown to fill the whole space. "Big as Quickthorn is, he couldn't help all of us escape. But with all of us shrunk down to such a small size, he could."

"She could have warned us," Sebastian grumbled.

"Maybe there wasn't time," said Quinn.

"So what now?" Tom said.

"I guess we need to see where this passageway leads us," Sebastian said.

"We don't have much choice," Elanor said. "Quickthorn is taking us that way, whether we want him to or not."

The unicorn was walking towards the dark arch, his horned head hanging in exhaustion, but still determined. Although the children were growing fast, they were still only just big enough to sit astride the beast's broad back.

"Where are you taking us, Quickthorn?" Elanor asked, stroking the beast's black mane.

Quickthorn gently raised his head in reply and looked back at her, whickering.

The arch led to a narrow passageway, winding up through the rock. Elanor blew on her ring so that light glowed, showing them the path Quickthorn was taking.

The passageway seemed to wind on forever. Before long, the children had returned to their natural size and had slithered down the unicorn's back to walk on either side of him.

It was cold and all their clothes were still damp. Elanor's gown was in tatters, the silk stained, the gold thread torn and dangling loose. Her slippers squelched with every step.

At last the passageway led out to a secret valley, lying in a hollow beneath high rocks. A round pool of water lay in the center, staring up at the sunset sky like a dropped silver coin. A stream wound its way from the pool to the lip of the valley and poured over it in a flurry of white water.

Around the pool grew silver birch trees, their trunks tall, thin and mottled black and silver. Under their shadows, short-cropped grass grew, with red-spotted toadstools growing in circles by their roots.

It was just on sunset, and the western sky was aflame with vivid colors. To the east, the full moon was just rising, huge and orange. As the children explored the small hollow, the colors slowly faded away and stars began to glitter in the sky. There was no other way in or out of the valley. It was perfectly hidden, circled by rocks.

"Fungus!" Tom cried, suddenly tripping and falling on his hands and knees.

Elanor rushed to his side to help him up. But she quickly dropped his arm, distracted by something half hidden in the grass—the dark object Tom had tripped over.

With a gasp, she picked it up and held it out for everyone to see. "I don't believe it . . . it's a unicorn horn!" She held the spiraling black horn in her hand.

"Unicorns must shed their horns in winter, like deer shed their antlers!" Quinn said. "Here's another!"

"Quickthorn brought us here so we could find one!" Elanor was glowing. "I've been worrying about how we were meant to get his horn without hurting him. Thank you!" She hugged the unicorn, then wrapped the gleaming black horn carefully and tucked it into her sack.

The sunset light seeped away. The air was cold, and Elanor rubbed her arms and wrapped the old shawl around her. There was something eerie about the silence of the valley, with the birch leaves in a constant flutter, and the faint mist rising from the pool.

Sebastian climbed up to the top of the rocks. "Such an amazing view," he called. "We're so high here, and the moon is so bright, you can see for miles over the forest. I can even see where the forest has been burned. We're really far away from it now."

"I hope Wilda wasn't caught," Quinn said.

"I hope she *was*," Sebastian retorted. "I don't trust her."

"Sebastian, get down," Tom called. "Lord Mortlake is still out there somewhere, looking for us."

Sebastian jumped down. "Even if he does see me, he'll never figure out how to get in here."

"He could send the bog-men up here," Tom pointed out. "They scuttle up like spiders, they'd have no trouble climbing the cliff."

Elanor turned back to the unicorn. He had waded into the pool, all silvered with moonlight, and was dipping in his horn. Droplets of water ran down his horn, as bright as mercury. Elanor was thirsty. She bent at the pool's edge and dipped her right hand in the water to take a handful. It was shockingly cold and her flesh turned numb at once. She was raising her hand to her mouth to drink when Quinn cried out, "Ela! Stop! Your hand!"

Elanor fell back on her heels and gazed down at her hand.

It had been transformed into solid silver.

FULL MOON,
DARK MOON

It was a long, unhappy night. They were all hungry, but there was nothing to eat but toadstools. They were all thirsty, but no one dared taste the enchanted water. They were all cold, for the pool breathed a frosty vapor that crept into their bones and made them shudder. They were all afraid.

Most of all, the four friends were shocked to the core by the transformation of Elanor's hand. From the wrist downward, it was stiff, heavy, cold silver, which clanged when accidentally knocked against a rock.

Quinn sat with her arm around Elanor, both shivering in their damp clothes. Sebastian sat nearby, his sword bare and resting over his knees. Tom stood, moving restlessly around the grove of birch trees, tearing strips of bark off the trees and twisting them into little hats before dropping them.

The moon slowly rose to the height of the sky. Quinn wished they could light a fire, but Lord Mortlake, his knights and his bog-men were still out there in the forest, looking for them. Lord Mortlake would see the fire's red glow and smell its smoke. He would find them.

"I'll read the tell-stones," Quinn said at last, reaching for the small bag at her waist. "Perhaps they can help us."

She drew four stones and laid them in a circle, and four heads bent over to see what she had drawn.

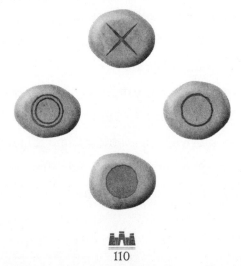

It was too dark, even in the flooding moonlight, and so Elanor tremulously blew on her moonstone ring so that a frail blue light shone out and they could see the symbols.

Crossroads. Full Moon. Dark Moon. Ring.

"I don't understand," Quinn said. "Full Moon means white magic, Dark Moon means black magic, Crossroads means a place of transition, a dilemma, and Ring means the coming of full circle—the end of one cycle and the beginning of another."

"It doesn't make any sense," Tom said.

Elanor lifted her cold, silver hand and let it drop with a thump. "No," she managed to say. Her face was white, her eyes were red. "Why did Quickthorn bring us here?" she asked again, for the umpteenth time. "I thought it was for the horn, but now I'm not so sure . . ."

The unicorn stood nearby, cropping the grass under the birch trees, a dark shape among the pale, slender trees. Behind him, the pool glimmered with that unnatural silveriness.

Quinn put the tell-stones away, then cupped the

wooden talisman in her hand. "Sylvan, are you awake? Please, can you wake up? We need your help."

The wooden eyes slowly opened. The Oak King gazed up at her. In the bright cold moonlight, his face was all grooves and shadows.

What troubles thee, little maid?

"Elanor . . . she touched the water of the pool . . . it has turned her hand to silver. What do we do, Sylvan? How can we fix it?"

Lift me so I may see.

Quinn lifted the wooden face so he could see Elanor's hand, so bright and hard in the moonlight, and the eerie pool of water.

The little maid touched the water?

Quinn nodded.

Was the beast washing his horn at the time?

Quinn nodded again.

Ah. I wonder . . .

"What?" Quinn begged him "Was it wrong to do that?"

"What is he saying?" Elanor asked. "What did I do?"

The beast's horn is magical, Sylvan said. *Like all wild magic, it is mysterious and unknowable.*

He was silent. Quinn felt his warmth, alive in her hand, his eyes hidden in shadows. Elanor stared at Quinn and Sylvan, waiting anxiously for an answer. Tom came to crouch next to her, patting her shoulder awkwardly.

Perhaps . . . said Sylvan. *I wonder . . .*

"What?" Quinn lifted the wooden face closer to hers, trying to read its expression.

What heals can harm, what harms can heal, Sylvan said at last.

"What does that even mean?" Quinn cried. The others tried to question her, but she held up a finger, bidding them to be quiet.

I will need to think on this, little maid. Let me think.

She couldn't get another word out of him, even though she shook him in her frustration. At last she let the talisman flop back down onto her dress, and told the others what he had said.

"Nothing but riddles," Sebastian said in disgust.

"I'm sure there's something we can do to fix it."

Tom tried to comfort Elanor, but she shook her head.

"There's nothing we can do," she said. "I'll have a silver hand for the rest of my life. It's my right hand too. I won't be able to write, or draw, or even cut my own food. I'll be utterly useless."

"Let's try and get some sleep," said Quinn. "Come, we'll try and keep each other warm. Things will look better in the morning. They always do."

Elanor lay down and lifted the edge of her shawl so Quinn could share it. The ground was cold and hard beneath them, and Quinn's feet felt like lumps of ice. She tucked them up in the hem of her gown as best she could, shut her eyes, and tried to think.

What heals can harm, what harms can heal . . .

Quinn woke in the morning to the sound of Tom's flute. Although it faltered and sometimes screeched, he was playing a familiar tune. Fergus sat nearby, his head cocked, one ear pricked, a baffled expression on his face.

Quinn sat up. Frost cast a lacy cobweb over her shawl. Her breath puffed white. It seemed impossible that it was midsummer.

Tom saw her sit up and lowered his flute. "We need to move on, Quinn," he said. "The days are getting away from us. If we don't find the griffin soon, and all the other beasts of the prophecy, we're going to fail. My mam . . . the Grand Teller . . . Lord Wolfgang . . . they need us."

"We've been in the forest for days," Elanor said, huddling in her shawl.

"We must be halfway through by now," Quinn said. "The story in Wilda's book said that the standing stones that led to the griffin's eyrie are in the heart of the forest."

Sebastian grinned. "I have a riddle for you."

"The last thing we need is more riddles!" Tom said.

"Just listen, it's a good one."

"Very well, what is it?" Quinn tried to keep her impatience out of her voice.

"How far will a blind dog walk into a forest?" Sebastian asked. Fergus looked up at the word "dog" and thumped his tail.

"That's not a riddle, that's a joke," Quinn said.

"Just wait till you hear the answer," Sebastian replied. "Come on!"

"Very well," Elanor said. "How far?"

"Halfway. After that he's walking *out* of the forest."

They all sat silently for a moment, thinking about this.

"Are we walking *out* of the forest now, without realizing it?" Elanor asked, her voice timid. "We have no way of knowing," she said. "We could be walking in circles, for all we know."

"What do we do?" Tom said.

"We can't give up the quest," Quinn said.

"But we need help!" Elanor cried.

Tom frowned and twisted the ring on his finger. His mother had given the ring to him before they fled the castle, Quinn remembered. It had something to do with his father. She remembered their last night at Wolfhaven Castle, when Tom's mother had told her son to seek his father in the forest. *You will find him where the wolves howl,* she'd said, and given Tom that ring. Tom had asked her how he was meant to know his father, as if he had never seen him before. *He has your eyes,* his mother had told him.

"What about your father, Tom?" asked Quinn. "Doesn't he live here in the forest? Your mam thought he'd be able to help us, didn't she?"

"She did, but, I don't know where to find him," Tom answered. "I've never met him. I know nothing about him."

"How can you know nothing about your father?" Sebastian asked.

"I just don't."

Sebastian opened his mouth to ask more questions but Tom, his face dark and scowling, took out his flute and began to play. His tune was shrill and wild, filled with anger and melancholy. Fergus stood up, whining. After a few more piercing notes, the wolfhound lifted his nose and began to bay.

The sound was met by the distant howling of wolves.

Tom stopped playing at once. He looked down at the flute in his hands, his face puzzled and afraid. He shoved it into his pocket.

"We're taking too long on this quest," he said at last. "We need to push on, we need to move faster!"

Quinn nodded. "I'm sorry. We shouldn't have stayed with Wilda for so long."

"Was she tricking us all the time?" Elanor's voice was desolate. "I mean . . . those Ellyllon creatures poisoned us and made us sick . . . and then she persuaded us to stay when we wanted to move on . . . then she shrunk us! And tied us to the unicorn who led us to this strange and horrible place."

"I don't know," said Quinn. "She looked after us when we were sick . . . she taught Tom to use his flute . . . and she saved us from Lord Mortlake and the fire. We could never have outrun him ourselves. There was no time for her to explain all of her actions."

Although Quinn defended the old, humpbacked witch, her voice was unusually hesitant. She felt troubled and unsure. Her hand went up to touch Sylvan's wooden face.

He had warned her. *Not all witches are wise,* he had said. *Not all hags are honorable.*

"There's no point worrying about it," Tom said. "What's done is done."

Elanor sighed, but got to her feet. The silver hand hung heavy and useless by her side.

"Now we need to work out how to get out of here," Tom said, as he gathered up his longbow and quiver of arrows.

They all paused, remembering the passageway that led down to the waterfall, and how the unicorn had leapt the chasm between the cliff and the cave. It was impossible for them to do the same.

"There's no way to get down the cliff face," Sebastian said. "It's far too steep. We'll have to jump down into the pool."

15

WOLVES IN THE NIGHT

"I'm not jumping," Elanor said, staring down into the foaming waters far below. "And I can't swim. I'll drown!"

"I'll go first," Sebastian said. "I'll be down there, and will be able to tow you out."

"I'm *not* jumping," Elanor repeated, squirming on the spot. "I can't!"

"You have to, Ela," said Tom.

"We have to get out of this place," Quinn said firmly. "If you stay here, you'll die."

"What if I ride Quickthorn out?" Elanor said. "He jumped in, he must be able to jump out!"

Tom slapped his head with his hand. "Of course!"

"And I could take all our clothes and weapons with me, so that they're not ruined by the water," Elanor suggested.

"Good idea," Quinn said, unbuckling her knives and passing them to Elanor. Tom and Sebastian followed suit.

Tom inched farther onto the narrow ledge that stood at the tip of the waterfall. Its thunderous roar filled his ears, and he was already wet from head to toe with spray. He looked down at the deep pool, then wished he hadn't. The drop was at least ten times his own height.

Beside him, Sebastian took a deep breath, closed his eyes, and jumped. He plunged into the water and disappeared.

Tom watched anxiously. As soon as Sebastian's head broke through the water, he gave a ragged cheer.

"Go now," Tom said to Elanor. "Good luck."

Elanor wheeled the unicorn around and rode it to the very back of the cave. "Jump high, please, Quickthorn," she whispered in his ear. "Jump far." Then she kicked him into a canter.

Quickthorn hurtled down the cave, then leapt through the waterfall, his front hooves tucked up to his chest, his hind legs extended out behind. Elanor crouched on his back, her head tucked low. Tom and Quinn rushed to the edge of the waterfall, to peer out past its hurtling white curtain, and watch the dark soaring shape.

When Quickthorn landed on the rock opposite, and wheeled to a halt, both Tom and Quinn cheered. In the pool below, Sebastian pumped one arm. Elanor waved her silver hand and it flashed in the sunlight.

Quinn jumped into the pool next. She came down like an arrow, her toes pointed, and scarcely made a splash as she hit the water. In seconds, she'd surfaced and was swimming strongly for shore.

Tom hesitated on the ledge above, his hand on Fergus's ruff, trying to pull him out past the waterfall's edge. The wolfhound dragged back against his hand, his ears low. Tom gave him another rub on the head, then turned and jumped over the cliff. Exhilaration shot through him as air whooshed past his body.

He hit the water hard, and plunged deep. Bubbles

burst up all around him. He curled his legs up against his chest, then, when his descent slowed, struck up strongly for the surface. As soon as his head broke free, he gulped air and looked up, calling to his dog.

Fergus barked, shrill and loud. Then he ran out a few steps, hesitated, looked over, then jumped too. His hairy body twisted and turned as he fell, and he hit the water with a massive splash. Fergus dog-paddled up to Tom, his head held high out of the water.

"Good boy," Tom said, rubbing his soft ears.

"What would you have done if he hadn't jumped?" Sebastian asked, wringing water out of his shirt.

"I knew he'd jump," Tom said, wading over to the pebbly shore. "He was always jumping into the harbor after sticks when he was a puppy."

Tail wagging, Fergus followed him and, of course, came as close as he could to Tom before shaking himself enthusiastically.

"Now we'd better work out which way is east," Tom said. "Elanor has the knapsacks—the compass is in there."

He waved at Elanor, riding the unicorn back down

the path towards them. She waved back and her hand flashed like a lantern.

"What can we do about her hand?" Quinn whispered.

"Nothing," Tom said. "There's nothing we can do."

Taking turns, once more, to ride on the unicorn's back, the four children moved as swiftly and silently through the forest as they could.

They were all hungry, and Tom was on the lookout for anything they could eat along the way. He found a wild apple tree, and they gathered handfuls, then hurried on, munching as they went.

They tried as much as possible to keep heading east, but the paths did not always meander that way and often the undergrowth was too tangled to push their way through.

Before nightfall, Tom found some mushrooms, picked bunches of wild sorrel, mallow and dandelion leaves, and dug up some burdock roots. Sebastian couldn't help teasing him about his habit of picking pretty flowers, but when Tom managed to shoot a rabbit and serve it up roasted that evening, with fried burdock, mushrooms and green leaves, he was not so quick to joke around.

"I have to eat my words along with the rabbit," Sebastian said. "Maybe cooking's not such a useless thing to know."

Tom gave a wry grin. "Even soldiers on the march have to eat."

He looked to where Elanor sat, shoulders slumped, her chin propped in one hand, her silver hand dangling from her knee. She looked pale and woebegone.

He took out his flute and tried a few notes. The flute felt more and more familiar in his hands, each time he conquered another note, or another tune. Tentatively Tom tried to play a lullaby his mother had always sung to him when he was a little boy. After a few false starts, he mastered it, and the sweet notes sung out.

Elanor lifted her head and gazed at him, eyes shining. She began to sing:

"Sleep, my babe, my heart's delight,
Sleep on through the darkest night,
Do not worry, have no care,
My darling child with hair so fair,
Close your eyes, shut them tight,
Darling baby cradled there."

Then, unexpectedly, came the far-off howling of a wolf. It rose, faint, eerie and undulating, into the night. Another howl joined it, and then another.

The unicorn reared and yanked against the rope that bound him to the tree. Fergus was restless and uneasy, nose lifted to sniff the wind.

Tom stopped playing. Elanor stopped singing. The four sat in silence, listening intently.

Slowly, the howling died away. There was only the soft shifting of leaves and the faraway call of an owl. The unicorn ran back and forth, ears laid down.

"Don't worry," Tom said. "Fergus will look after us."

The wolfhound had been sitting upright, listening, his ears pricked and all the hair on his spine quivering. At the sound of his name, he turned his head and thumped his tail on the ground.

Sebastian threw more wood on the fire. "Wolves don't like fire," he explained.

"They sound a long way away," Quinn said in a comforting way. "Tom, could you play that song again?"

Tom hesitated, then played it again softly.

"My mother used to sing that to me," Elanor whispered. "Every night she would come and sit on my bed and sing to me. I'd forgotten. It's been so long . . ."

She tried to wipe away a tear, only to bang herself in the face with the clumsy silver hand. She winced in pain. "Oh, I hate this!" she cried. "I want my hand back! I want my home back! When will this be over?!"

Quinn knelt beside her, hugging her. "We'll find the griffin soon, never you fear, and the dragon and the sea serpent too."

"It's impossible!" Elanor cried. "It's *crazy!*"

"No, no, it's not. We've found the unicorn, that's proof it's not impossible." Quinn smoothed back Elanor's tangled hair.

"And now he's made my hand turn to silver."

"I'm sure he didn't mean to," said Quinn. The unicorn whickered gently from the shadows, and bowed his horned head. "See?" Quinn added.

Elanor wiped her face with the sleeve of her gown.

"Here, use this." Sebastian passed over a folded square of cotton, rather crushed and grubby-looking. Elanor wiped her eyes and blew her nose and tried to smile. "Sorry," she said, tucking the handkerchief into her bodice.

"Well, we do need to think about where we're going," Sebastian said. "Do we even know what we're looking for?"

"The stone gateway," Quinn answered, "that looks like a griffin."

"To the east," Tom said.

"That's all we know," Quinn said. "It's not much, but . . ."

Tom was silent. *And maybe . . . my father . . .* he began thinking. The thought gave him a fizzing sensation in the pit of his stomach. "You'll find him where the wolves howl," his mother had said.

Tonight, the wolves had been howling in the east.

THE WILD MAN OF ⟩⟩⟶
⟵⟨⟨ THE WITCHWOOD

All day, they trudged through the forest.
Tom's stomach felt like a hollow cavern.
Though he saw a few birds and some rabbits, he wasn't
quick enough and all his arrows fell awry.

The children argued nearly all day, over stupid
things—whose turn it was to ride the unicorn . . .
whose fault it was that no one had thought to bring
a fishing line . . . over whether or not to light a fire
that evening.

"What's the point?" Tom asked. "We've nothing
to cook on it."

"I'm cold," Elanor said. She sat on the ground,
her chin resting on her hunched-up knees. "Quinn,

I think the silver's spreading. My arm is all numb and tingling. Look!"

Elanor held out her arm, and sure enough the warm flesh of her arm from wrist to elbow was streaked with silver. She was shivering so hard her teeth rattled.

"What if my whole body turns to . . ." Elanor couldn't finish her sentence. She hugged her arm tight, as if she could stop the spread by keeping it warm.

They all sat, staring at Elanor's arm, then Sebastian got up. "I'll find us some firewood."

They made a fire and sat beside it in the twilight, toasting the last of their apples on sticks. Elanor looked pale. Quinn tucked her up in the shawl and brought a warm rock for her to rest her feet on. Sebastian promised to travel the world, fighting trolls and ogres, till he'd found the cure.

Tom turned his mind to the Oak King's riddle. *What heals can harm, what harms can heal.* "Maybe," he thought aloud, "we need to find some poisonous plant, like the foxglove, that can also be used to heal."

"Foxglove made me feel so sick, I don't want ever

to feel that again," Elanor said.

The flames made a friendly crackling sound and warmed their faces and hands. Once they had eaten, everyone began to feel better, though it was not enough. Not nearly enough.

"What I wouldn't give for a hot pigeon pie," Sebastian said.

"Spiced pear and butterscotch pudding," Quinn said. "With cream."

"Roast goose with sage stuffing," Elanor said.

Tom could not bear it. He groped for his flute. "No more talking about food," he said. "Come on, Ela, how about a dance instead?"

"A dance?!" Elanor scoffed. She lifted her silver hand and let it fall.

"It's your hand that's turned to silver, not your feet," he told her. "Come on! I've had enough of this moping."

Tom got to his feet and began to play a jig. "Come on!" he urged again, jumping side to side like a jester.

Sebastian laughed and began to tap his foot.

"How can I dance around when my father is a

prisoner?" Elanor flared. "When my arm is turning to silver!"

"Better than sitting around moaning," Tom said.

"Let's dance tonight because tomorrow we'll find the griffin!" Quinn cried, leaping up. Her bare feet were quick and sure on the ground, her white skirts swirling. "Get up, Ela!"

"Do you really think we will?" Elanor gasped. "Find the griffin tomorrow, I mean."

"Yes!" Quinn cried. "If not tomorrow, the day after. Arwen would never have sent us on this quest if she hadn't believed we could do it. We have to trust her . . . we have to trust ourselves."

Suddenly Sebastian jumped up. "I'll show you all how it's done!"

To everyone's great surprise, he began to dance around the clearing. He snatched up a stick from the woodpile, and began to tap it against the trees as he hopped past. The girls clapped, and joined in his madcap dance. Holding hands, they spun and bowed and turned forward and back, before collapsing on the ground in fits of laughter as the song came to an end.

"At Ashbyrne Castle," said Sebastian, "all the men dance with bells and sticks. My father was the best of all! You should come and see him one day—"

Sebastian suddenly sobered and fell silent. He threw his stick to the ground so hard that it cracked in two.

"I should have sent my father a message," he said. "I should have ridden for him at once. He would send men, if only he knew."

"There was no way to send him a message," Quinn said. "It all happened so fast. And those bog-men were everywhere."

"He'll think me a fool." Sebastian sat down, all the laughter gone from his face.

No one knew what to say.

Tom lifted his flute to his mouth again. Without really planning to, he played a lament. The music soared into the air. As he played, Tom thought of his own father. If they met, would his father think him a fool too?

A wolf's howl rose into the night.

Another wolf answered it.

Both were close by.

Tom kept on playing, and was answered by a crescendo of howls, surrounding them on all sides.

The unicorn was frantic, neighing and bucking and plunging. Elanor ran to him.

"Stop playing, Tom!" she cried. "You're drawing them to us!"

But Tom ignored her. He kept blowing into the flute and the howls came closer.

"What are you doing?" Sebastian leapt up and tried to snatch the flute out of Tom's hand. Tom rolled swiftly away, and leapt to his feet, still playing.

Sebastian lunged at him, but Tom dodged away again. It was as if a spirit of wickedness had possessed him, as if he was driven to danger by some impulse he couldn't control. Sebastian kept trying to grab him, but Tom made it impossible.

"He's calling the wolves to us," Quinn said.

The sound came again, chilling and wild. It rose and fell, throbbing with menace. Fergus raised his hackles and stared into the darkness, snarling.

"Please stop," Elanor pleaded. "Please, Tom!"

Tom ignored her. He played like a madman in the firelit darkness. Sebastian stopped trying to catch him, and listened to the howling of the wolves, the growling of the wolfhound, and the lilting of the flute.

"We need help," Quinn said. "Maybe Tom's father can help us. Maybe he knows where the griffin is. Maybe he can help us fight Lord Mortlake. Maybe this is what Tom's supposed to do!"

"Maybe we'll get ripped to shreds by the wolves first!" Sebastian snapped back.

They were all on their feet now, looking into the dark forest. It was late and the moon was riding high in the sky. The flickering firelight made everything seem unsteady and dangerous.

Tom kept on playing, drawing the wolves to him. He felt, in some deep secret part of him, that it was the only thing to do.

Would the wolves bring his father to him? Tom wasn't sure he actually wanted to meet him. His father had left when Tom was only a little boy, and had never come back. For years Tom had wondered about him and tried to imagine what he was like, but gradually—realizing how his constant questions upset his mother—Tom had stopped asking.

But, still, he kept on playing the flute. It felt right. The howling no longer terrified him, but filled him with exhilaration.

Then Elanor gasped. She pointed a shaking finger.

Green points of eyes stared at them through the shadows. Here and there, the flickering firelight showed the shape of a muzzle with bared jaws, or a head with pricked ears.

Fergus was growling, deep in his throat. His hair stood up all along the length of his spine. His teeth were bared.

The wolves slunk closer, their eyes gleaming. Every now and again, one flung back its head and howled. The clearing was alive on all sides. Sebastian drew his sword. "Look what you've done!" he said to Tom. "We're surrounded!"

Suddenly Fergus lunged forward, seizing a wolf by the ruff. The two animals rolled over each other, biting and snarling. Tom dropped his flute and ran, but as he tried to drag the wolf off Fergus, it turned and snapped at him. Tom shouted in pain and wrenched his hand away.

It was red with blood.

Other wolves leapt to attack, and Fergus was dragged down by a dozen snapping jaws and heavy-muscled furry bodies. Tom picked up a length of wood and swung at the wolves, shouting his dog's name. Elanor screamed and tried to get to Fergus, but Sebastian held her back. Quinn pelted the wolves with apples, but they did not even look around. Fergus yelped. The unicorn reared.

Suddenly another figure was amongst the pack, as shaggy as a wolf, running on all fours, snarling and biting. Yet he was not a wolf—he was a man, dressed in a wolf pelt, with long boots of hide. His hair and beard were gray and hung in filthy elflocks. His lips were drawn back in a snarl.

He snapped at the wolves and bit their ears and muzzles, and dragged them away from Fergus with a heavy stick shaped like a claw.

The wolves fell back and slunk away. Fergus rolled over and got up, limping. He licked at the wounds on his shoulders and haunches. Tom was shaking. He bent and grabbed his flute, he hardly knew why.

"Is it the wild man?" Sebastian whispered.

The man was growling at the wolves and pushing them aside with his shoulder. One turned and licked his face, and he licked it back.

Tom stared at the wild man, remembering how he had warned him that danger was in the wind. The wild man stood up, turning, shaking back his matted gray hair. Tom saw the grime engrained in the lines on his weather-beaten face, saw his black, broken nails, and the flash of gold on his finger.

Taking a deep breath, Tom looked into the wild man's forget-me-not blue eyes, and said, "I think you may be my father."

HUNTER'S CAVE

"Yes," the wild man said.

Tom couldn't speak. He felt no joy at the discovery, only shame. His father was dirty and shaggy and lived wild in the forest with wolves. Tom looked away, swallowing hard.

"Come," the wild man said. "There are many enemies in the forest. Come with me."

Tom shook his head.

"It is not safe here."

Tom shook his head again.

"I have food."

Tom would not look at him.

"I said, come with me!" the wild man roared,

making everyone jump. He seized Tom by the arm.

Tom did not look at the others. He shook his arm free, bent and caught up his knapsack and weapons.

"That is my old bow," the wild man said. "Can you shoot it?"

Tom allowed himself a bitter smile. "Not very well."

"I will teach you." The wild man kicked dirt over the fire, smothering it. "Come," he said to Sebastian and the girls. "Bring the beast. I shall not let him be hurt."

Silently everyone gathered up their belongings and followed him. Elanor lead the skittish unicorn, soothing him with hand and voice. Fergus limped along beside Tom, his tail sunk between his legs. Every now and again he looked into the shadows and growled, and a wolf would growl back.

The wild man moved so swiftly and easily through the forest, that everyone had trouble keeping up. In his wolf pelt, he was almost invisible in the marbled shadows. Many times, he had to stop and wait for them. Tom did his best to move as quickly and silently as his father, but every cracking twig and rustling bush sounded like an ax blow.

At last they came to a clearing by a great rocky bluff. The wild man led them into a cave that he'd made comfortable with wolf pelts. He'd built a fireplace and stone chimney against one wall, the smoke staining the wall all the way up to a crack in the roof above. All kinds of dried fish and meat hung from the ceiling, and baskets filled with roots, nuts and seeds lined the wall.

A wolf cub lay sleeping on furs by the fire. It sat up when the children came in and yawned widely, showing needle-sharp teeth. Fergus stopped in his tracks, hackles rising, but the cub bounded over to greet him, jumping up to lick the wolfhound's nose then rolling over to show him a creamy belly. Insulted, Fergus stalked over to the fire and lay down by it, heaving a great sigh.

Silently the wild man gestured at the pelts. Worn out, the children sank to the ground. They were very aware of the wolf pack which lay down on the ground at the cave entrance, eyes fixed on them in suspicion and curiosity. Quickthorn was uneasy, his ears flicking back and forth, his body tensed and ready to flee. The wild man opened a sack of wild oats for him, and the unicorn began to feed, tail relaxing.

The wild man then threw wood on the fire. It blazed up, filling the cave with warmth and light, and making the wolves' eyes gleam. With a stick, he swung an old black cauldron onto the heat.

"Dog first," the wild man said. He busied himself making a paste out of some kind of herbs and tallow, and then tended the bloody bites on Fergus's shoulders and haunches. The wolfhound lay quietly under his hand, even beating his tail in response to a rough caress on his head. "He remembers me," the wild man said.

Tom was angry. "How? How could he remember you?"

"I gave him to you."

"You did? Fergus? When?"

"Before I left. He was just a pup, but I handled him a lot. He would know my scent."

"He's only eight years old. How could you have given him to me?"

"You were five when I left. You don't remember me?"

Tom's face grew hot. "No."

"It was a long time ago." The wild man moved to Tom's side, tending the angry wolf bite on his hand with the same herb and tallow mixture he'd used on the dog. Tom wrenched his hand away.

"Yes, it was," said Tom. "So why did you leave? Why abandon me and Mam to come out here, to live in a cave with a dirt floor, with a pack of wolves?"

"You and your mam were fine. The wolves, though, they were hunted unto death." The wild man took Tom's hand again and tended it gently, wrapping it in cobwebs, and then in linen bandages torn from the boy's shirt. Quinn watched him with great interest, though both Elanor and Sebastian looked repulsed.

"I thought you were meant to hunt them, being the Royal Wolf Catcher?" Tom said.

"Yes," his father said. "I hunted the wolves. I killed them. But the time came when I could kill them no more." As he spoke, he rose to tend the meal. "Let's eat."

All this time, Sebastian, Quinn and Elanor had sat quietly, wide-eyed, listening to the quick exchange between father and son. At the mention of food, they all sat up eagerly. Elanor, forgetting for a moment her silver hand, held up both hands to receive a bowl of stew. The wild man saw her gleaming metallic hand and took a step back in surprise.

"I dipped my hand into the water where the unicorn was washing his horn," she said, tucking it away under her skirt. "It turned to silver. I'm afraid my whole arm, the whole of me, will turn silver too. Do you, by any chance, know a cure?"

"No, sorry," he answered. "That is a question for a witch."

Elanor heaved a deep sigh. She took the bowl of stew from him, propped it on her lap, and ate clumsily with her left hand. The others followed suit eagerly. No food had ever tasted so good.

The warmth of the fire, the nobility of the wolves—who lay quietly, listening with alert ears and eyes—and the deliciousness of the venison stew all helped them relax and begin to feel drowsy.

"Thank you, sir," Elanor said, as the wild man took her empty bowl.

"My name is Hunter," he replied.

"Thank you, Hunter," she said, and Sebastian and Quinn echoed her. Tom said nothing. His hand was throbbing, his head was aching.

Hunter took his bowl. "Your mam understood. She forgave me."

When Tom did not answer, Hunter squatted beside him. He pointed at the golden ring Tom wore, then showed his own ring. The first was forged to represent two hands holding a heart. The second was forged in the shape of a crown. Hunter yanked his ring off his finger and took Tom's finger, sliding his ring down so it nestled against the ring Tom wore.

Tom shook his head and looked away, covering the double ring with his other hand. Hunter sat back and shrugged, his weathered face troubled. "All any of us can do is what seems right."

"Hunter . . ." Quinn said hesitantly. "We need

help. Do you know what has happened?"

Hunter shook his shaggy gray head. "I knew there was danger. The wolves smelled danger. I did not know what."

"Wolfhaven Castle was attacked by Lord Mortlake, the lord of Frostwick Castle. He has used some kind of black magic to raise dead men from the bog."

Hunter frowned. "And Lord Wolfgang?"

"He was taken." Elanor's voice shook. "Everyone was taken."

"Everyone . . . but us," added Quinn. "We escaped. We've been sent on this quest and we're trying to save them, the best we know how, but it's been hard . . . dangerous . . ."

"We're being hunted." Sebastian took up the tale. "We rescued the unicorn from Frostwick Castle, but Lord Mortlake wants him back. I don't really understand why . . ."

"The unicorn heals," Hunter said. "In war, that is a great gift."

Tom leaned forward, his frowning gaze suddenly intent on the unicorn. *What harms can heal, what heals*

can harm. He remembered how Lord Mortlake's wife, Lady Mortlake, had wanted him to kill the unicorn so his horn could cure her headache. He remembered how the unicorn had been washing his horn in the water when Elanor had dipped in her hand to drink. He wondered . . .

Quinn explained to Hunter how they hoped to awaken the long-ago heroes, said to sleep under Wolfhaven Castle, with the help of a unicorn's horn, a griffin feather, a dragon's tooth and a sea serpent scale.

Hunter's frown deepened. He looked troubled.

"A griffin is said to live in the heart of the Witchwood. Have you ever seen one? Do you know where it might be?" Quinn gazed at the wild man hopefully.

He shook his head. "Never seen any such creature in these woods."

Quinn sighed. "Wilda, the witch of these woods, had a book with a story about a man who helps a griffin. It described his journey through a gateway shaped with the head of an eagle and the haunches of a lion. The sun is meant to shine through it on midsummer morn."

Hunter hesitated a long moment, then said reluctantly, "I do know of a place that could be described that way. It is a fell place, though, and not one I'd like such young ones to visit."

"We must," Elanor told him. "Our friends and families are all being held prisoner. We have to do whatever we can to help them. Before it's too late . . . I just wish we knew we were following the right path."

Hunter sat silent, thinking. The wolf cub had crawled onto his lap and fallen asleep. Hunter tugged its ears and smoothed its rough coat, before saying, "Very well. I will take you there tomorrow. Sleep now. You are safe here."

The children all lay down by the fire, covering themselves with the warm pelts. Hunter waited till they were all settled, then stood up, the wolf cub in his arms. He bent and laid it down next to Tom.

"For you."

18

MIDNIGHT ATTACK

Elanor woke slowly. Her body was warm and snug, but her arm was heavy and cold and tingling with pins-and-needles. She opened her eyes and lifted her arm. It was silver to the elbow.

Elanor let it fall down, and laid her other arm over her eyes, trying not to cry. She imagined the silver slowly spreading over her skin, reaching for her heart with bitter claws, filming over her eyes. How long till she was silver all over? Would it hurt?

"Look!" Quinn's shout caused Elanor to sit up. She looked to see where Quinn was pointing. With a sudden kick of her heart, she saw that Tom was asleep by the fire. Lying next to him was Fergus, his wolfhound, head resting on his paws. Snuggled up in the curve of the wolfhound's belly was the wolf cub.

"*When the wolf lies down with the wolfhound,*" Quinn said softly. "It's the first part of the prophecy! It's come true!"

Tom sat up sleepily, pushing his fair hair out of his eyes. When he saw the dog and the wolf cub curled up together, his eyes went wide.

"It's a sign," Quinn said. "Now I *know* we'll find the griffin!"

Sebastian jumped up and buckled his sword to his belt. "Let's get on the road! The sooner we find the griffin, the sooner we can get back to the castle!"

Tom bent and ruffled the wolfhound's ears, hiding his face. When he looked up, his blue eyes were bright. *I was right to bring us here*, he thought to himself.

Quinn was shaking her crumpled skirts, and buckling her daggers. "Sebastian's right, let's go."

They all looked so happy and relieved, Elanor didn't have the heart to show them her silver arm. She pulled down the hanging sleeves of her dress, then, awkwardly, pulled on her slippers. As Quinn helped her buckle her dagger, Elanor looked over her curly black hair, searching the shadowy reaches of the cave. "Where's Quickthorn?" she asked.

Tom's face was grim. "And where's my father?"

Together the children raced outside and a dozen wolves leapt to their feet, hackles raised, fangs bared. Menacing growls rang out.

"Good boys," Tom said, holding out both hands in a calming gesture. "Quiet now."

The growling intensified. One wolf stepped forward, stiff legged, muzzle raised to sniff at Tom's hands. Tom stood very still.

A warning bark sounded out. Elanor looked around. Hunter was loping swiftly towards them. He barked again, sounding exactly like a wolf. At once the wolves stopped growling. Their hackles sank and their tails began to wag. Hunter growled at the one who had sniffed at Tom's hands, and it whined and crouched down, its tail sinking between its legs. Hunter knuckled its head and neck, still growling, and the wolf rolled over and exposed its pale belly. Hunter let it lick his hand.

"Quickthorn?" Elanor asked. "Where's our unicorn?"

Hunter pointed down to the river. The unicorn stood, hock deep in the water, drinking. At the sound of Elanor's voice he lifted his head and looked around, then nodded his head in greeting, his black mane blowing in the wind.

As they set off through the forest with Tom's father leading the way, Elanor kept close to the unicorn's side, stroking his neck with her good hand.

The wolf cub gamboled with them, pouncing on fluttering leaves and wrestling with twigs, making everyone laugh. Fergus kept close by Tom, the hair stiff along his spine, all his attention focused on the wolves slinking through the forest with them.

The path narrowed, and Tom and Sebastian had their usual roughhouse over who would walk first. Hunter stood silent, frowning, till they stopped.

"Too noisy. You must learn to walk silently and leave no trace. Look." He showed them the snapped twigs and scuffled dirt their altercation had caused. "Too easy to track."

He broke off one of the twigs and lightly swept it

over their footprints. He then showed them how he stepped from stone to stone, or on the hard verge of the path, so he left no print in the soft soil. Both boys tried to mimic him. He nodded. "Good."

A little farther on, he halted them with a raised hand. Then he beckoned Tom forward and quietly pointed out a hare grazing in a small clearing some distance away. He indicated Tom's longbow. Tom drew the string and aimed carefully, but the arrow fell uselessly in the grass, some distance away from the hare. The animal leapt in the air and sprinted away but, quick as a thought, Hunter drew his bow and fired an arrow after it.

The hare fell at once and Hunter strode to retrieve it, hanging it over his shoulder, before retrieving Tom's fallen arrow and returning it to him.

"You must practice," he told Tom.

For the rest of the day, Tom shot constantly—at whorls in the trunks of trees, at birds flying past, at small beasts scuttling into the shadows. He missed them all. His frustration made his aim even wilder.

"Anger makes you shake," Hunter said. "You must

be calm to shoot well. Keep your wrist steady. And you grip your bow too tightly. Think of your bow as a living thing. You do not want to bruise it. Keep your hand gentle and kind. That's it. Now try."

This time when Tom shot, the arrow sang straight into the knot in the tree that he'd been aiming for. By the time twilight fell over the forest, he'd caught a brace of wood pigeons.

Hunter spoke little, but every word was a caution or a lesson. Elanor was amazed by how much he knew about the forest. He foraged as he walked, as Tom had done, but knew a use for every single tree or plant they passed. He taught them not to strip a bramble of all its berries, or a tree of all its nuts and fruit, but to make sure they left enough for the other creatures.

He harvested flax stems and taught Sebastian how to braid them into a fishing line, then made a fishing weight from a stone and birch bark. He rubbed the wood pigeons with thyme leaves, juniper berries and wild garlic, then roasted them on a spit over the fire, with mushrooms, leeks and burdock roots. Elanor thought it was one of the most delicious meals she'd ever eaten.

Hunter shared the hare with Fergus and the wolf cub, and left the wolves to hunt for themselves. Quickthorn cropped the long grass.

After the wolf cub had eaten his fill, he staggered over to Tom and climbed into his lap. "Does he have a name?" Tom asked his father.

"Wulfric," Hunter told him. "It means 'wolf strength.' His mother was killed by a bear a few months ago. I've raised him since."

"Wulfric," Tom whispered to the cub. Wulfric lifted his muzzle and yawned widely, showing rows of tiny sharp teeth.

As they ate, the children told Hunter of all their adventures and Quinn asked him what he thought of the witch Wilda's actions.

"She kept us from traveling on, and then she made us as small as ants," Quinn said, her voice troubled.

"Best to keep still after foxglove poisoning," Hunter said. "Takes a few days to recover."

"Well, that's what she said, but . . ."

"Foxglove strains the heart," Hunter said. "The heart can give out if overtaxed."

"So she meant it for the best?" Elanor asked.

"A witch guards the forest as best she can. If she thought you meant to hurt the forest or its creatures, she would have let you die from the poison. But she let you live."

Elanor glanced at Quinn and smiled, relieved. It had hurt to think she'd betrayed them.

"What about shrinking us?" said Sebastian.

Hunter shrugged. "You said you were being hunted. The unicorn has no scent. It is why they are so hard to catch. The witch was throwing your hunters off your trail."

"Quickthorn has a scent," Elanor said indignantly.

"What does he smell of?" Hunter said.

"The forest," Elanor said.

"Yes. He does not smell like a beast. If he did, I would have trouble keeping my wolves from trying to tear him to pieces. But they barely notice he is here."

Elanor thought about this. It was true. For wolves, their primary sense was that of smell, and so an animal without a scent must be virtually invisible to them.

"Why don't they tear Fergus to pieces?" Tom asked.

"Dogs and wolves are brothers. They should not hunt each other, and so I have told them."

Fergus thumped his tail. Wulfric was lying between his paws. He thumped his tiny furry scrap of a tail too, and licked the wolfhound's muzzle.

"Now sleep," Hunter told them. "You will need all your wits about you tomorrow."

Elanor was so tired from the long day's march through the forest that she was glad to lie down by the fire. It wasn't long before sleep overtook her.

She was woken some time later by the howling of the wolves. The sound was met by a terrible baying sound, like wild dogs set loose.

Elanor sat up, clutching her shawl. "What is it? What's the matter?"

"The hunter has found the hunted." Tom's father seized her hand and swung her up. "Get up, get your things. You must flee."

Tom was already up, pulling on his hat and his boots, catching up his bow and quiver of arrows.

Sebastian had his sword bared in his hand, staring into the night.

"I will stay and fight them. Me and my wolves. You go on. Quickly now. Head due east, into the light of the rising sun."

As he spoke, Hunter filled Tom's knapsack with food. He threw the knapsack to Tom who swung it onto his shoulders, then lifted first Elanor and then Quinn onto the back of the unicorn.

"Go!"

Quickthorn galloped down the path, Sebastian and Tom running fast beside them. Fergus and Wulfric streaked along behind.

Elanor risked one quick look back. She saw the giant boar race into the clearing, tusks swinging viciously. Behind him rode the black-armored knights on black horses, hooves thundering. One wore a helmet crowned by the tusks of a boar.

"Lord Mortlake," she whispered, then bent over the unicorn's back, urging him on faster.

19

GUARDIAN
OF THE GATE

Sebastian ran, his breath rasping in his chest. The sun was rising in the east, and birds everywhere were screeching madly. Tom ran beside him, and ahead the unicorn galloped, the two girls clinging to his back.

The sound of battle had faded away. It seemed impossible, though, that one man and a pack of wolves could have prevailed against so many armored knights and the giant boar. Sebastian's throat felt thick, and his eyes burned. Every now and again he raised a hand and dashed it across his brow, wiping away sweat.

Elanor drew Quickthorn to a halt and pointed with her silver hand. "Look," she whispered.

Ahead, the pathway led down into a narrow gully. On either side of the entrance were two great pillars of stone. Each was shaped by the forces of wind and water, into a curving hook. It was easy to see a resemblance to an eagle's beak. Below, the base of the pillars spread into what looked like a lion's powerful haunches. The path led between the pillars towards a great archway of stone that led into a cliff.

"We're here. We've found it." Quinn spoke in a low voice.

"Let's go!" Sebastian pushed forward, but Tom caught his arm.

"Wait," he whispered. "Look at Fergus."

The wolfhound was growling, his nose pointed forward, one foot lifted. By his side, the wolf cub mimicked his stance, tiny hackles raised.

"What's that rumbling sound?" Tom whispered.

The two girls slid off the unicorn, and they all tiptoed to the pillars together, peering around the rock. It felt like the ground was trembling.

For a moment the valley was still and quiet, but then the rumbling returned. Sebastian suddenly realized that what he had thought was a giant craggy boulder resting against the cliff was, in fact, a giant.

A two-headed giant.

The giant's two heads were both snoring, eyes shut, mouths wide open. The sound of their snores whistled and boomed through the gully, their immense gray beards flapping up and down with each snore.

"We have to get past him . . . *them*," Tom said. "Maybe if we're really quiet . . ."

"He might be big, but I bet he's slow," Sebastian said, drawing his sword. "I'm sure we could beat him in a fight."

"Really? Look how huge his hands are. He could squash us with a single blow." Quinn pointed at the giant's immense hands, resting on his stomach.

"Maybe if we galloped past on Quickthorn's back, we'd be too fast for him to catch us," Elanor suggested.

"Quickthorn couldn't carry all four of us," Tom pointed out. "Not if he was galloping fast, anyway."

"Let's try to go quietly then," Quinn said. "And if the giants wake up, we'll run as fast as we can."

Tom bent and picked up the wolf cub, tucking him

under one arm and putting his hand over his muzzle. Tom did not want anything to wake the giant.

Slow step by slow step, the children crept down the gully. Quickthorn led the way, his feathered hooves ringing slightly as they hit the stone. Tom stopped him and took one of the old sacks, tearing it into four with the help of his dagger. He tied the sacks around the unicorn's hooves, so that when Quickthorn stepped out, his hooves made no sound. Sebastian suddenly wondered if Lord Mortlake had muffled the hooves of his horses in the same manner on the night they had attacked Wolfhaven Castle. It would explain how eerily quiet the invasion had been.

Closer and closer they came to the giant. He was ten times as tall as Sebastian, and almost as wide as he was tall. His spread legs were like felled tree trunks, his clenched hands like boulders. Sebastian could not take his eyes off him.

Suddenly Sebastian tripped and fell flat on his face. His sword hit the ground with a clang.

The giant woke with a jerk and a snort. All four

eyes opened, and he rubbed first one set, then the other, with his immense and hairy hands.

"Fee-fi-fo-fum, I smell the blood of humans," one of the giant's heads roared.

"Be he live or be he dead, I'll grind his bones to make my bread," the giant's other head roared.

"Run!" Tom shouted.

They all ran. Elanor, the smallest and youngest, and weighed down by her heavy silver arm, soon fell behind. Sebastian turned and grabbed her hand and helped her run. Quickthorn wheeled and came back for them, and Sebastian flung Elanor up on the unicorn's back.

A giant foot thudded down next to his head. Sebastian swerved, but was almost squashed by the second foot thumping down. He drove his sword into it, and the giant bellowed and shook his foot. The sword fell out, bringing with it a little trickle of dust. Sebastian snatched his sword again, as the giant bent and swept Elanor up in his enormous hand, lifting her towards one of his mouths.

Quickthorn whinnied and stabbed the giant in the

leg with his horn. The giant shrieked and stamped, and the unicorn stabbed him again in the other leg. The giant yowled and hopped around on one foot. Dust swirled out, filling the air. Tom fired arrow after arrow, but they only reached as high as the giant's ankle.

Sebastian drove his sword deep into the giant's big toe, then used it as a step to clamber up on top of the giant's hairy foot. He had to grab hold of the giant's hair to stop himself being thrown off. The giant shook Elanor back and forth and her long golden-brown hair whipped around wildly. She screamed and struggled.

Sebastian grabbed hold of the long hairs on the giant's legs and used them to haul himself upward.

"Fee-fi-fo-fum, I smell the blood of humans," one of the giant's heads roared.

"Be he pink or be he blue, I'll mash his flesh to make my stew," thundered the other.

He lifted Elanor to his mouth, but then she punched him in the nose as hard as she could with her silver hand. He yowled and dropped her, sending her tumbling through the air.

Sebastian, now halfway up the giant's chest, reached out with one arm trying to catch her. But he couldn't reach her. She plummeted past. "Ela!" he cried.

Just before she hit the ground, the giant's other hand caught her.

"Fee-fi-fo-fum, I smell the blood of humans," one of the heads said.

"Be he far or be he near, I'll boil his blood to make my beer," said the other.

Elanor was lifted, struggling and fighting, back towards the giant's mouth.

Quickthorn reared and slashed the tip of his horn across the back of the giant's knee.

The giant crashed down to the ground.

At once, Sebastian was up and running. He bolted up the giant's chest, caught hold of one long gray beard, and began to climb. He reached the giant's chin just as he opened his mouth and crammed Elanor in. Sebastian jammed his sword in, stopping the giant from closing his mouth, and hauled Elanor out. Together they slid and slipped and slithered down the giant's long beard, all the way to the ground. The giant flailed and thrashed, but could not get the sword out.

Sebastian reached the ground and lifted Elanor down. "Let's go!" he shouted. Hand in hand, they ran for the cave. Quinn darted past them.

Sebastian looked back to see her swiftly pluck three hairs from the giant's beard. Then she turned and was belting down the gully towards them, the hairs streaming out from her hand like wiry, gray ribbons.

The giant struggled to his feet and ran after them, each step making the gully shake and shudder, boulders crashing down to the floor. He gnashed his teeth in fury, snapping Sebastian's sword in two. His great hand swooped down towards Quinn.

Tom fitted his last arrow to his bow and raised it high. With a twang, the arrow sprang free. It soared straight towards the giant's eye and pierced it through. The giant screamed and clapped one hand to his face.

Quinn bolted through the archway and into the cave. "Come on!" she cried. "Let's get out of here!"

20

PATHWAY OF GOLD

"That was a great punch!" Sebastian said.

"Who would have guessed my silver hand would prove so useful?" Elanor replied with a shaky smile.

Quinn smiled at her. "What a battle that was. It should go down in history as the greatest battle against a two-headed giant ever."

"You could write it all down for us," Elanor said. "When we've saved everyone at Wolfhaven Castle."

Quinn's green eyes turned dreamy. "Maybe I will."

The four children were trudging down a narrow track that wound through a series of caves, many of them as huge as the great hall of the castle. They had been walking for at least three hours, but dared not stop. Quinn had a vision of the two-headed giant tearing the cliff to pieces, trying to reach them.

Their way was lit by the eerie bluish glow of Elanor's moonstone ring. It glittered on quartz embedded in the rock, and the occasional slimy trickle of moisture running down from ceiling to floor.

Quinn's feet were icy, and she wished for a thick shawl like Elanor's. She huddled her arms around her and her fingertips brushed against the three hairs she had plucked from the giant's beard. She wondered what mad impulse had led her to do such a thing. Perhaps, she thought, it was the story she'd read, in which three hairs from a giant's beard proved of magical help.

"I hope my father and the wolves escaped," Tom said in a low voice. "Do you think . . . do you think he could?"

"Of course," Sebastian said. "That old man of yours is as tough as a nut. He'll be fine."

Tom tried to smile.

The day passed slowly, and at last the children had to rest. They slept in a row, their heads cushioned on the unicorn's flank, their feet warmed by the wolfhound and the wolf cub. It was pitch-black in the cave, so they had no sense of what time of day or night it was. Hunger woke them in the end. By the light of Elanor's ring, they chewed on dried venison and tried to quench their thirst with berries. On they walked, following the path ever downward.

At last the track led them to the shores of a lake. Although the lake was hidden within an immense cavern, the roof overhead had fallen in, letting light pour in. The light was clear and golden, the first light of day. It lit up the thin veils of a lofty waterfall, falling down from the lip of the cliff, and created a dazzling golden pathway that led to the tall island of rock in the center of the lake.

An eagle's cry rang out and Quinn's heart leapt. Squinting against the blaze of light, she peered at the island, which was made of massive fallen boulders of stone. At its peak was a straggly nest of sticks and moss. Within this eyrie was an immense golden eagle, with a curved beak as long and sharp as a scythe.

"Wow, look at that eagle," said Quinn, awed by its immense stature.

All four admired it from afar, when suddenly the bird reared up, and revealed the mane and hindquarters of a great lion.

"The griffin!" they cried out at once.

The griffin shrieked again. Quinn's heart was hammering so loud she felt it bruise the bones of her chest. She had not imagined the beast would be so huge or so terrifying.

"How on earth do we reach it?" Sebastian asked. "It's a long swim and a high climb."

"And if we do reach it, how on earth do we get a feather?" Elanor said. "It'll kill us if we get too close!"

Tom simply shook his head, overwhelmed.

Use the giant's hairs, little maid. Sylvan spoke in Quinn's mind. Startled, she touched him with one hand. "What? How?"

Think, little maid.

Quinn untied the giant's hairs from her waist and looked at them. They hung limp from her hand, dirty and gray, thick as rope. She looked around her. The shore of the lake was bare rock. Tom was pacing impatiently, bending to test the temperature of the water with his filthy, bandaged hand, then picking up a stone and skipping it out along the pathway of gold. Sebastian was rolling up his sleeves, preparing to dive in the lake. Elanor sat wearily, slippers kicked off, hugging her silver arm.

Quinn remembered how she'd thrown the tell-stones a few days earlier. She had drawn out a stone with the symbol of the Crescent Moon painted upon it, a sign of new magic and intuition. At the time, she'd wondered if the stone had been trying to tell her to use her intuition. If so, she had failed to listen.

Up till now. Quinn bent and touched Elanor's slipper with the end of one of the giant's hairs. At once it began to grow and change. Within seconds it had transformed into a golden boat with a curved prow. The giant's hair shriveled and turned to dust.

Elanor cried out in amazement, and the boys turned around.

Laughing, Quinn touched the other slipper. Soon it too had transformed into a golden boat, and the second giant's hair had dissolved and blown away. Quinn, Tom, Fergus and Wulfric climbed into one, while Elanor and

Sebastian together coaxed the unicorn into the other. Drawn by some invisible current, the two boats glided across the lake towards the great column of rock.

"I'm not such a bad witch, after all, hey, Sebastian?" Quinn teased.

"Not bad at all!" he responded with a grin. "Though you'd really impress me if you conjured up a new sword for me!"

The golden boats reached the shore and Tom scrambled out. "Now to tame the griffin!"

"But how?" Quinn demanded. "It could kill you, Tom."

"I thought *you* were the riddle master," he teased. "Don't you remember what Sylvan told us, about how to catch the griffin?"

Quinn shook her head. "It was so long ago." Sylvan spoke again in her mind and Quinn repeated it:

At the sound of me, women may dance

Or sometimes weep.

At the sound of me, men may dream

Or stamp their feet.

At the sound of me, babes may laugh

Or drift to sleep.

At the sound of me, beasts may come

and their master greet.

"But what does it mean?" Elanor cried.

Sebastian scratched his curly red head.

Tom drew out his flute. "Don't you get it? The answer is *music*! Music can do all of those things. It was music that called the wolves to me."

Tom tucked the flute into his pocket and began to climb. "Be careful, Tom," Elanor called. The two boats had turned back into shoes, and she had to grab them out of the water before they went bobbing off.

It was a tough climb. Tom almost slipped and fell a few times. Fergus whined and stood up on his hind legs, putting his front paws up on the rock. Wulfric tried to mimic him, but his legs were much too short, and he fell down. Fergus came down to all fours to nuzzle him and lick his face.

Quinn craned her neck, hands clasped together in anxiety. Sebastian was tense and impatient, wanting to climb up after Tom, and only prevented by Elanor clasping his arm.

At last Tom reached the eyrie. The griffin shrieked and took to the air. Tom almost lost his grip as the wind from the huge golden wings beat against him. The griffin circled, a streak of gold in the shining air, then swooped for him, talons raking. His curved beak slashed down, the claws of his hind legs raking for Tom's belly. His tail was as fast and cruel as a whip.

Tom leapt into the nest, grabbed the flute from his pocket, and began to play.

Sweet music lilted into the air. The griffin soared away, then swooped down again. Tom kept playing. The griffin circled again, then came down to rest on a rocky outcrop next to Tom. His front talons could have sliced Tom's head from his body. His beak could have gouged out Tom's eyes or gashed open his throat. His powerful claws could have gutted him with a single slash.

Yet the griffin did not slice or slash or gouge or gash. He slowly crouched down and laid his head on Tom's shoulder.

Tom dared not stop playing.

A loud rumbling, grumbling noise rose from the

griffin. Quinn tensed. Tom played faster. The rumbling and grumbling noise continued.

After a long, tense moment, Quinn recognized the noise. "It's all right, Tom. He's purring!"

21

◄ THE ►
GOLDEN FEATHER

Tom lowered the flute. The griffin cocked his head and stared at him with bright, fierce eyes. Slowly, Tom put out one hand and stroked the bird's magnificent golden feathers.

The griffin nudged Tom's hand with his beak. Tom played him another tune, even as he looked all around him. The nest was woven from old branches and moss and mud. Here and there, bright golden feathers were caught in the twigs. Tom stopped playing long enough to gather as many as he could. He stuck one long wing feather in the brim of his hat, and tucked the others inside his pocket with his flute. *For the poor old blind witch*, he told himself.

The griffin was watching him closely. Tom stroked his neck again, then moved his hand down to the golden fur of the griffin's back. The beast was warm under his fingers. The griffin was easily as big as the unicorn, though his front half was feathered and his back half was furred. The griffin gave a little beckoning jerk of his head. Tom stroked the curve of his neck, then—greatly daring—climbed on his back.

The griffin bowed his head for a moment, then spread his wings and launched into the air.

Tom held on tight with his legs and hands as the griffin soared and swooped above the lake. From below came the cries of his friends. He waved at them, but then clutched the griffin's neck again as the great beast dived down towards them.

The griffin slowed and stopped on a rock beside the lake. Tom slid off his back. His legs almost gave way beneath him. His friends stared at the pair in disbelief.

Tom steadied himself, then took off his hat and showed his friends the long, golden feather.

The girls jumped up and down, laughing. Quinn

ruffled Tom's hair and banged his back, and Elanor kissed his cheek. Sebastian shook Tom's hand vigorously. "You did it!"

The unicorn and the griffin regarded each other curiously, then Quickthorn bent his head and bowed, one foreleg outstretched, his horn almost touching the ground. The griffin bowed in return.

"I need a name for him," Tom said. "What's something that means king?"

"Rex?" Quinn suggested.

"Perfect!" Tom stroked the beast's golden feathers and once again the deep, rumbling, purring sound arose.

"I found some extra feathers," said Tom, showing the feathers in his pocket. "I thought we could try and find that old witch Wilda and give one to her. To see if it helps heal her blindness."

"Thank you, Tom," Quinn said warmly.

"Now we just need to find a way out of here," Elanor said. She looked up at the hole in the roof of the cave. It was a long way above them.

"I can fly the griffin," Tom said. "But you . . ." Tom stopped and looked at Quickthorn.

"Even if the griffin let *us* on his back with you, we can't fly Quickthorn out that way," Elanor said.

Quinn was clutching the last hair of the giant's beard, dangling from her belt like a filthy rope. "Elanor, give me your belt," she said.

Surprised, and eager to see what Quinn was going to do with it, Elanor unbuckled her belt. It was made of overlapping golden links like the scales of a snake. Quinn laid it on the ground and touched it with the giant's hair.

It began to writhe and twist with a terrible rattling sound. The griffin spread his wings and flew away, much to Tom's despair. The belt reared its buckled end, squirming like a giant snake. In moments, it had transformed into a golden stairway that climbed from the lake up to the rim of the cliff.

They all began to climb the stairs, the unicorn pacing along gravely. Elanor picked Wulfric up and carried him in her arms.

Tom trudged behind. Those moments on the griffin's back had been so exhilarating.

The griffin swooped past, shrieking. Tom had an idea. He pulled out his flute and played it.

The griffin flew close, wings spread, hovering. Tom grinned and leapt once more onto his back.

Away they flew, boy and griffin, spiraling up towards the dawn-bright sky.

Left behind on the golden staircase, Fergus whined, his ears and tail drooping. "Come on, boy," Elanor told him, rubbing his rough head with her one good hand. "Never mind."

It was a steep climb and took ages. At last Sebastian stepped off the golden staircase and stood, head hanging, panting.

"Took you long enough," Tom said from the top of the cliff.

Sebastian looked up. Tom was resting against a log by a pool of water, his blue hat tipped over his gleaming blue eyes. "Fine for you," Sebastian replied rather sourly.

"Isn't it?" Tom laughed. He jumped up and grabbed Sebastian's hand, thumping him on the shoulder. "Come and sit down. I've cooked breakfast."

"Good on you!" Sebastian came forward eagerly.

Quinn was next, looking white and tired, but

happy. The oak medallion hanging around her neck had his eyes wide open, and he seemed to be smiling. Quinn suddenly laughed and patted him with her hand. Tom guessed he'd spoken to her, in her mind.

What astonishing powers the Grand Teller's gifts proved to have! Tom glanced for a moment at Sebastian's dragon brooch and wondered what magic lay hidden in the glowing amber. As if hearing his thought, Sebastian put up his hand and touched it, a look of longing on his face.

But then Elanor climbed up, Wulfric cuddled in one arm. The other arm hung silver and useless. Beside her Fergus trotted, shaggy tail waving, and behind her stepped the unicorn, his horn glinting in the morning light.

Tom bit his lip, wondering. He'd had a mad idea the other night, listening as Quinn had told his father about all their adventures. It had been such a rush ever since—escaping Lord Mortlake, fighting the giant, taming the griffin—that he'd had no time to think about it further.

But now was the time. It was sunrise and moonset,

the pool before them glimmering with delicate colors. Tom scooped up a pot full of water and took it to the unicorn. The unicorn looked at him gravely with large dark eyes, then bent his head and dipped his horn in the water. Tom then put the pot down and washed his hands in the water. It was cold and tingly and made him gasp.

He then slowly unwound the stained bandage on his hand. The wolf bite below was completely healed. He flexed his hand and took a deep breath. "Elanor," he called.

She came towards him, her brow knotted with weariness and anxiety, her hazel eyes troubled. "What is it?"

"Wash your hand in the pot."

Tentatively she held out her good hand, grubby, with chewed nails, and dipped it in the water.

"No, no, the other one!"

Elanor glanced at his face, curiously, then slowly dipped her stiff silver hand in the water.

After a moment or two, she was able to flex it. Face radiant, she raised her eyes to Tom's face, then looked again at the water. With growing excitement, she splashed the water up her arm, rubbing it in furiously.

When she drew her hand out of the water, it was warm flesh once more.

"I'm healed!" she cried. "Look!"

"*What heals can harm, what harms can heal*, Ela!" Tom said.

Once again everyone cried out in amazement. Elanor skipped around the clearing, lifting her green silk skirts. "Thank you, Tom, thank you!"

Carefully Tom rubbed some of the enchanted water on Fergus's wounds, till they too were healed, then poured the rest into the waterskin. "For my father and his wolves," he explained. "I'm sure they must be hurt."

Everyone sobered. Hunter had stayed to fight Lord Mortlake and his knights, one man and a pack of wolves against a whole battalion of soldiers. Not to mention that huge and hideous boar, and the bog-men.

"We'll go and find him now!" Elanor said, seizing the bowl of food Tom had made for her and shoveling it into her mouth in a most unladylike way.

"And we'll give Wilda a griffin feather to cure her blindness," Quinn said eagerly.

"Then," Sebastian cried, "we go in search of the dragon. Agreed?"

"Agreed!" the others cried.

They set off into the brightening morning, the two girls riding on Quickthorn's back, Sebastian running alongside with Fergus and the wolf cub at his heels. Tom soared overhead.

From Rex's back, Tom could see for miles. He'd never realized how huge the world really was. It shook him in a way he had not expected. He guided the griffin lower, searching, but it was impossible to see anything through the canopy of leaves.

Tom gripped tightly to Rex's back with his knees and drew his flute out of his pocket. It was a huge risk, but he began to play. With both hands occupied with the flute, he was unable to hold on to the griffin. The great beast flew on steadily, however, and Tom played with all of the longing in his heart.

A wolf howl rose from the forest and Tom's heart

thumped. As he played on, more howls sang out. Tom grinned and guided the griffin down to follow the white cascades of the river. There was the clearing, and the steep cliff honeycombed with caves. There was Hunter, sitting on a rock, trying to bind the many gashes on his bare chest and arms. His skin was streaked with blood, one eye so swollen he could barely see. Wolves pressed close all around him, licking their wounds.

"Father!" Tom cried.

Hunter looked up. Gladness filled his face and he jumped to his feet, waving.

Tom threw down the water bottle. "Healing water," he called. "From the unicorn's horn!"

Hunter caught it deftly, then flung back his head and howled in gladness and triumph. Tom laughed, and howled back. All the wolves below lifted their muzzles and joined in. The eerie sound echoed through the quiet forest.

"I must go," Tom shouted through his cupped hands. "I'm sorry."

"The wolves and I will meet you at the castle,"

Hunter shouted. "We'll fight with you. Ring the bells and we shall come!"

"Thank you!" Tom waved his hand in acknowledgment.

"Keep safe."

"And you!"

The griffin soared away. Far below, Tom saw the unicorn galloping, Sebastian running full speed beside him. Tom gestured with his hand, telling them where to go. From high in the sky, he could see the black scorch of the spent wildfire, the black branches of the ruined ash tree. He flew down and saw the witch, Wilda, sitting in the smoldering ashes of the clearing, her face and arms streaked with soot. She was rocking back and forth in grief, a fox cub limp in her arms.

The griffin flew low and Tom drew out a golden feather from his pack. "Wilda!"

The witch struggled to her feet, her blind eyes searching the sky. "Who? Who calls my name?"

"It's Tom. I'm up here. I found the griffin! Here, catch!" He dropped the golden feather for her, but it slipped through her fingers and fell to the ground.

She dropped to her knees, searching through the hot ashes, till her groping fingers found it. A cry of triumph broke through her. She brushed the feather across her milky eyes.

Tom watched in amazement as two white discs fell from the witch's eyes. She looked up, eyes bright as sword points. She raised a bony finger and pointed at him. "I see you, Tom Pippin! I see you!"

Tat-tat-tat.

Tom's heart lurched. He looked down.

A bog-man crouched in the smoking branches of the ancient ash tree. His nostrils flared as he caught Tom's scent. He beat his spear relentlessly against the tree's blackened trunk. *Tat-tat-tat.*

Tom urged the griffin high into the air as suddenly, from all around the burned-out clearing, arrows came whizzing towards him. He saw archers hiding by every tree, their bows held at the ready. Higher and higher the griffin flew, so high the arrows could not reach them.

Tat-tat-tat.

The sound echoed through the shadowy tangle of

the Witchwood.

Tat-tat-tat. Tat-tat-tat.

Bog-men ran through the forest, banging their spears as they caught Tom's scent. Tom could only hope that his friends could outrun the bog-men. He bent over the griffin's neck, calling to him, "Fly faster, Rex, faster!"